# CALL OF THE KING

### RISE OF THE KING
### BOOK ONE

# TJ GREEN

Call of the King
Mountolive Publishing
©2020 TJ Green
1st edition 2016
2nd Edition published 2017
All rights reserved
ISBN 978-1-99-004700-8

Cover Design by Fiona Jayde Media
Editing by Sue Copsey and Missed Period Editing

To Jason, thank you.

"Or how should England dreaming of his sons
Hope more for these than some inheritance
Of such a life, a heart, a mind as thine."
– Alfred, Lord Tennyson (1809–92)
  *Idylls of the King*

# Prologue

One evening towards the end of summer, Jack strolled down the path to the bottom of his garden, pushing through the heavy vegetation that crowded in on either side. The air was thick with pollen and heat, and bees buzzed drunkenly around him. He rested his elbows on the gate and leaned his weight against it, feeling his pruning clippers push into his hip. He lit his pipe, narrowing his eyes against the smoke, which he blew around him in an effort to drive off the midges that now appeared in the twilight.

Beyond the gate a stream trickled by, and here the air was cooler. It smelt earthy and damp; he could feel its sharpness on the back of his throat.

Jack's knees and lower back ached. He'd spent too long in the garden, and he was too old to cope with it as he used to. He rubbed his cheek and felt the stubble. He could almost feel the grey in it, as if it were coarser than in his youth.

The silence was disturbed only by the stream, and the wind easing through the trees. He breathed deeply, savouring the cool and the smoke. Shadows slanting through the trees cast the banks into darkness, so that he could no longer easily distinguish between the trees, the banks, the rocks, or the stream.

He started singing an old folk tune, and as he did, saw

something stir at the foot of the gnarled yew tree across the stream. Were his eyes playing tricks on him? It looked as if a figure was moving, as if someone was stirring from a long, deep sleep. Maybe what looked like long limbs were in fact tree roots thrown into relief by the shadows, and what looked like a face was a knot in the trunk? But then the figure moved again, and legs and arms became distinct. With a jolt, he realised he was looking into two unblinking eyes, fixed upon him with an unexpected intensity.

Jack's singing faltered and he blinked rapidly, several times. The figure moved its head as if it were a snake, its eyes glittering before blinking languorously. It rose in one swift movement and became a man. No, not a man, but something that looked like a man—tall and slim with the grace of wind through tall grass, or water over stones. He was dressed in shades of green and a long cloak fell from his shoulders, almost to his feet, shimmering like a low mist.

And Jack knew what it must be, and that all of the stories from his childhood were true.

# Chapter 1: The Visitors

Tom raced down the garden path, jumped over the stream, and entered the wood, finally skidding to a halt in a pile of wet leaves.

He looked around, desperate to see the two people he'd seen watching the house, but the wood was silent, and there was no one in sight.

He shouted, "I know you're there, I saw you! Show yourselves!"

Nothing moved, and his words hung on the air like his frosty breath. He turned slowly, but the wood was still and silent, and Tom kicked the nearest bush in frustration. He knew they were out there, but they were unwilling to reveal themselves.

Tom took deep breaths in an effort to calm himself down, and unclenched his tight fists. It was only minutes before that he had been looking out of his granddad's kitchen window and saw the lurking figures, and he'd had the strangest feeling that they were there because his granddad was missing.

Reluctant to leave, Tom shouted again. "Come on! Talk to me! What do you want? Please!"

But again, there was only silence.

He looked around tree trunks and poked at thick,

scrubby bushes, covering the small area closest to the stream quickly, but after a few minutes, he had to admit defeat. Surely they couldn't have hidden themselves that quickly? Maybe he was seeing things.

Almost a year earlier, his grandfather, Jack, had disappeared with no trace of where he could have gone, and leaving his family confused and increasingly worried. They had investigated as much as they could before running out of options. The police had barely done anything because his granddad had left them a note to explain his absence. As far as they were concerned, that meant he was fine, and in theory, he was; the note was calm and rational. But he hadn't contacted them since, and that was just odd. But Tom hadn't given up. His granddad had to be somewhere, and someone had to know something.

Frustrated, Tom took a final look around and decided to return to the house, but as he turned his back, he felt a prickle of awareness. Someone was still watching him. He called over his shoulder, "You know where I am if you want me!"

He marched towards Granddad's cottage, where he was living with his father. They had moved in over six months before when it was clear his granddad wasn't going to return, and that his parents' marriage wasn't going to survive. The cottage was home now, and everything there reminded him of his grandfather and his mysterious disappearance. Tom opened the back door and entered the large kitchen-come-sitting room. He kicked his boots off, and put them on the hearth next to the roaring fire.

He shivered, holding his hands close to the flames. It was cold out, and this morning had seen a heavy frost. They were days away from Christmas, and the school term was over. A small pine tree signalled the season, but that was the only decoration they had put up. Without his mother there, neither he nor his dad had bothered with anything else. They hadn't even managed to change the house. It was exactly as his grandfather had left it.

Tom looked around the room, noting the old fashioned furniture, the worn armchairs in front of the fire, and the painted wooden cupboards that comprised the kitchen-half of the room. This was the heart of the house. There was also a small living room, but his grandfather had spent most of his time in here.

Tom's gaze drifted to his granddad's note that still sat on the end of the mantelpiece under a blue striped bowl containing spare keys, screws, pins, and other odds and ends. He picked it up, his eyes running down the page. He had told them very little, only that he was going away with a new friend and not to worry. Not to worry! His granddad was exasperating. He'd never known his granddad go anywhere before, but his dad told him he'd travelled a lot when he was younger. Maybe he had been bored and wanted a change. But who was his new friend? And why hadn't he told them his name?

A knock on the front door disturbed his thoughts, and then a voice shouted, "Tom, it's just me!"

It was his cousin, Beansprout, who at 15 was about a year younger than him. She was called Beansprout because of her skinny frame, but her real name was Rebecca. She barrelled through the door, her long, strawberry blonde hair swinging, and grinned. "Hey, Tom. My mom sent me over with mince pies." She set the old biscuit tin down on the table and narrowed her eyes at him. "Why are you looking at granddad's note? Have you found out something?"

He shook his head. "Not really. I thought I saw some people watching the house from the wood." He jerked his head towards the back of the house. "I think I'm just imagining things. Stupid, really."

He dropped into the chair by the fire and watched the crackling flames, feeling a wave of sadness wash over him. In all likelihood, he'd never see his granddad again. He just had to accept it. All he could hope was that he was safe and well somewhere.

Beansprout slumped in the opposite chair and stared into the fire, too. "It sucks, doesn't it? I miss him, too. Mum refuses to talk about it anymore. It upsets her too much."

"What a weird thing to do, to just go, leaving everyone behind. What kind of 'new friend' could make you do that?" Tom asked. He could recite the note by heart now. He'd examined every word, trying to find meaning in nothing.

Beansprout sighed. "It must be someone very special to make you leave your family. Unless he was taken by force?"

Tom barked out a laugh. "Why would anyone kidnap Granddad? We've not had a ransom note, either!"

"Sorry. Just pointless thinking—again." She stood and brought the biscuit tin over, and sitting again reached in for a mince pie, then handed the box to Tom. "Here you go."

He helped himself and munched silently, thinking of how he'd felt in the wood. "What if I'm not imagining things?"

"What do you mean?"

"I honestly felt as if I was being watched out there. If they were just dog-walkers, I'd have seen them! Why would they hide? That seems mad."

"Maybe they'd already walked on."

Tom shook his head. "I raced over there! They were

hiding when I saw them from the window, ducking behind tree trunks, especially that massive yew."

"Maybe you are right, then. Maybe they are here about Granddad!" Beansprout started to get excited. "Perhaps they have some news!"

"But why wouldn't they talk to me? Why hide?"

"Maybe they want to break in?"

Tom looked sceptical. "In the daylight?"

"Maybe it's a secret organisation?" Beansprout's eyes were wide with intrigue.

"That's one of your nuttier ideas," he said, finishing the mince pie and reaching for another.

"And you have a better one?"

Tom contemplated telling her what he'd been thinking for ages, but his idea was worse than hers. However, there was a reason he got on with Beansprout more than his other cousins, more even that his younger sister, and that was because she was open to all sorts of interesting ideas. He summoned his courage and asked, "What if he's somewhere else?"

She paused. "What do you mean?"

"No one's seen him or heard from him! You'd have thought he would phone, or email, or write a postcard! But there's been nothing for well over a year! He disappeared at the end of the summer! No one's found a body either!"

Beansprout grimaced. "Tom! That's gross."

"We have to be realistic! He's been gone for ages. Why wouldn't he get in touch? That means he's either dead, or somewhere else!"

"And by that you mean—"

He faltered. "Not in this world."

Beansprout feel silent, watching him, a myriad of

emotions running across her pale, freckled face. "That's quite a wild suggestion."

"I know."

"Is this because of your dreams?"

He shrugged, uncomfortable that she'd brought them up. "Sort of."

"Are you still having them?"

"Yes. Almost every night now."

Ever since their granddad had disappeared, Tom had been having strange dreams, and over the past few months they had been getting more and more frequent.

"Remind me what happens in them," she said, attentive.

"I see a woman with long, silvery hair who tells me to hurry up, that I'm needed. Sometimes I see a sword, lots of water, and then I get this feeling that I need to do something."

Beansprout leaned forward. "And they don't change?"

"No! That's what's really weird! Dreams are never the same all the time. This one is."

"You're sure you don't know who it is? Are you sure she's not been on the TV?"

"No! I think she's trying to communicate with me."

"You'd think she'd pick an easier way, like the phone."

Tom absently chewed his pie. "Exactly! I think she doesn't phone because she can't!"

"But does she ever mention Granddad?"

"No."

"So how are they connected?"

"Because this only started when he disappeared!" Tom said, his voice rising.

"All right! Calm down." Beansprout brushed crumbs off her sweatshirt. "Okay, if you're so convinced, let's go for a walk and try to find your visitors."

"Now?" He looked towards the windows. "It's already getting dark."

It was past three in the afternoon, and at this time of year, the daylight ended early.

Beansprout looked at the window too, frowning. "Okay. Tomorrow? Your dad's still at work, isn't he?"

Tom nodded. "He's working long hours. He's never back until late now."

Beansprout looked around the kitchen, concerned. "What are you eating?"

"Microwaveable dinners, why?"

Her shoulders dropped. "Why didn't you say so? Come to our house. There's always loads of food."

Tom shrugged. "Nah. I'm fine. The football's on."

Her face creased with worry. "Are you sure? Aren't you lonely?"

"Not really. Besides, whoever I saw earlier might come back."

"Don't open the door tonight. You might be attacked!"

"Beansprout, stop worrying! You're as bad as my mother. Let's go searching tomorrow. We could go for a walk, maybe as far the old folly in the middle of the wood. It's unlikely whoever it was will still be around, but you never know. I've always wondered if it's somewhere Granddad may have gone, too. We might find a clue. What time?"

The old folly was a derelict tower that had seen better days, and was a good walk from the cottage.

"Tenish? I'll bring some cake in my backpack."

"Okay. I'll make sandwiches." He smiled. "Cheers for this. It will make me feel better. At least we'll have tried to find them. I'm sure someone was there!"

She smiled, too. "It's okay. I feel as useless as you do, and I'd like to feel like we've done something. But it's freezing outside. I'll be very surprised if anyone's there now." She stood and headed to the door. "I better go—I've got some shopping to pick up. Are you sure you don't want to come for tea?"

"Sure. See you tomorrow."

# Chapter 2: A Sign

The next morning was bright and clear, and Tom woke early, jolting out of an unsatisfactory night's sleep. He'd had another dream about the woman with long, white hair. She whispered his name to him. "Tom, it is time." But she never said anything else, and when he tried to answer, she'd faded away, and the dream evaporated.

Time for what? She was always so vague. That was the nature of dreams, though. Weird, half-finished things that meant nothing and went nowhere. He was frustrated with himself for even thinking they meant something.

He'd dreamt about water, too, and the glint of something shining deep down beneath the shifting waves where he couldn't see it clearly. Sometimes he saw a bright blaze of firelight, and heard a low, murmured chanting that became louder and louder until it roared in his ears before receding like a tide. And sometimes when he woke up, it felt like someone had punched him on the birthmark at the top of his arm.

Shrugging it off, he lay in bed, looking forward to the day that stretched before him. He had no idea what he might find, or even what to look for, but it would be good to have company. He'd already packed his backpack with spare socks, a jumper, and bottles of water, and the sandwiches he'd made the night before were in the fridge.

He jumped out of bed and went to look at an old map on the bedroom wall. It showed the surrounding land as it had been over a hundred years ago. The cottages along the stream, including Granddad's, were marked, but the fields and farmland behind them were now covered in houses. The extensive woods across the narrow stream remained unchanged and were still surrounded by fields. Just visible at the top edge of the map was the small village of Downtree, also virtually unchanged since the map had been made.

Marked on the map, in the centre of the wood, was the strange, tumbledown stone tower that he and Beansprout would walk to today. Mishap Folly had been built more than a hundred years ago by the owner of the manor house. It was so-called because of the series of disasters that had overtaken the owner: the manor had been damaged by fire, crops had failed, and the owner's son had died after been thrown from a horse. Then the owner himself had disappeared and was never seen again. The tower had stood empty over the years, beginning to crumble as the woods encroached on all sides.

Tom estimated it would take a couple of hours to walk there. It was unlikely that Granddad had passed that way, but it had always annoyed Tom that so far, no one had checked it out. The police had been so dismissive at the time, and it annoyed him now just to think about it.

He pulled on his jeans, T-shirt, and jumper, and ran down the stairs. After putting some bread in the toaster, he opened the back door and took a deep breath as the cold, crisp air came flooding in. As he stepped outside he noticed an odd-shaped package on the doorstep. How had that got there? The postman never came to the back door.

He grabbed the parcel as if it might suddenly disappear,

and looked towards the wood, immediately thinking of the figures he had seen the day before. He had seen someone! He scanned the trees again, and then turned back into the kitchen to examine the package, shutting the door behind him.

The outer wrapping was a lightweight piece of bark, and as he lifted the edges, a gauzy material shimmered beneath it. He unfolded it to find his grandfather's watch and a note. Tom gasped, his head whirling with surprise. Behind him the toaster popped loudly, and in shock he dropped everything onto the table. Cross at himself for being so jumpy, he frowned at the toaster as he pulled the note from under the watch. It was Granddad's writing.

> *Sorry for the delay, but I've been very busy!*
> *I've sent you my watch, as it doesn't really work here, but I wanted you to know that I'm all right.*
> *I probably won't be coming home, so I hope someone is looking after the house and garden.*
> *I miss you all, but I know you'll be fine.*
> *Don't try to find me!*
> *Love, Granddad xxx*

The letter was written on thick parchment-like paper, and he wondered if there was some sort of secret message in it, but after reading the note several times, was sure there wasn't. Tom felt hugely relieved to know Granddad was fine. And then he felt really annoyed. What did he mean, 'Don't try to find me?' How ridiculous. Where on Earth was he? He kicked the table in frustration and buttered his now cold toast, itching to leave as soon as possible.

When Beansprout arrived, she was as mystified as Tom.

She propped her own bulging backpack against the table and examined the package while Tom rinsed his plate.

"This is bark, Tom! Who wraps a watch in this? It's just odd. Perhaps he's run out of money and is living off the land, like Robinson Crusoe?"

"And his Man Friday has brought us a present? I doubt it. Besides, he said he doesn't need his watch where he is, so he must be somewhere else! Just like I suggested yesterday. If he was here, close by, he'd see us."

"So who brought this?"

"The people I saw yesterday. I knew I was being watched!"

She stared at him warily. "This is uncanny. It's giving me goose bumps."

"And I had another dream."

"I've got a bad feeling about this."

"Why bad? It's clear he's okay. That's his writing!"

"What if someone made him write it?"

Tom shook his head. "Okay. This is getting us nowhere. Someone left that here last night, and they might still be here, so grab your bag. Let's go."

Beansprout glared at him, but changed the subject. "Are you going to leave your dad a message?"

"What did you tell your mum?"

"Just that we're going out for the day, and I'd see her this evening."

"Cool, I'll do the same."

He scribbled a note and left it on the kitchen table, then put the contents of the package in his backpack, just in case.

The wood was a tangled mass of bare tree limbs, and the ground was carpeted in dead leaves. Satisfied that no one was in close proximity to the cottage, they walked on into the heart of the wood, and an ever-increasing thicket of branches. For a while they didn't speak, spooked by the stillness around them, and both wary in case they were being watched. The only sound was their ragged breathing and the occasional crack of a twig breaking.

It wasn't until Tom spotted the roof of the folly through the trees that he broke the silence. "I can see it, we're nearly there!"

They quickened their pace, finally emerging into a clearing. The round tower loomed above them, its stone walls cracked and crumbling, its roof jagged. The ground was littered with broken stones. Moss had spread like patchwork, and ivy snaked up the walls until there was barely an inch of grey stone to see.

"Wow!" said Beansprout. "I didn't know it was so big!"

Tom nodded. "It's bigger than I remember, actually. And it's more ruined, too. What was I thinking? As if anyone would want to stay here! Especially Granddad. I'm an idiot. I actually thought he might be in there, smoking his pipe next to a fire."

Beansprout laughed. "That's desperation for you. Don't worry, Tom. I think we've all imagined all kinds of unlikely things."

"You check the inside, and I'll look round the back," Tom said. "Be careful!" he added as he tripped over a snaking branch of ivy.

"Yeah, yeah," he heard her mutter as she made her way to the entrance. "I'm not a child!"

When Tom reached the far side of the structure, he

peered around him at the trees, the tower, and the debris on the ground, and all at once felt stupid. It was ridiculous to even think he could find Granddad, or the person who had brought the package. Annoyed with himself, he huffed, and thumped back against the wall before sliding to the forest floor, his backpack squashed behind him.

Without a whisper of noise, a tall figure emerged from the wood and walked towards him, stopping a few feet away. It was a young man, just a few years older than Tom, with long, dark hair and pale skin. There was something different about him that Tom couldn't quite put his finger on. He wore a loose, pale-grey shirt and black cotton trousers tucked into leather boots. A long, thick grey cloak hung from his shoulders, almost reaching the ground. But what was unnerving was the sword tucked into a scabbard at his side, and the longbow and arrows visible over his shoulder.

He stared at Tom, and then sat cross-legged on the ground.

"Greetings. My name is Woodsmoke." His voice was soft and low, with a strange accent.

Surprised, Tom said, "Er, Hi."

"And you are?"

After debating whether telling this stranger anything was a good idea, he said, "Tom."

Woodsmoke nodded, as if that was the answer he'd been expecting. "I know your grandfather."

Tom's head shot forward, his mouth open wide. "How? Have you seen him recently? Is he all right?"

Woodsmoke laughed, so gently it sounded like rain on a roof. "So many questions, Tom. You remind me of him. He's fine. He doesn't want you to worry about him. That's why I brought his watch for you."

"It was you? And you were in the wood yesterday! But where is he? I want to see him. So much has happened since he left, he could help—I know he could."

"He's too far away to help. As he said in his letter, he won't be coming back. Whatever it is, you'll have to manage on your own. You aren't alone, are you?" Woodsmoke looked concerned, as if he'd misunderstood.

"No, I live with my dad. But..." He shrugged.

Woodsmoke sighed with relief. "That's good, then."

"I want to see him anyway!"

"I'm sorry, that is not possible. I shouldn't be speaking to you...I should have just gone." Woodsmoke looked cross with himself. "I must go, I have a long way to travel, and you must go home, too. Stop worrying, your grandfather is fine, that's all you need to know." He rose swiftly to his feet, but as he turned to leave, a woman came running around the side of the tower.

"Woodsmoke, quickly—the girl has gone into the tunnel."

"You said you'd sealed it!"

By now Tom was on his feet and looking at both of them. "What girl? Do you mean Beansprout?" But Woodsmoke and the woman were already running back around the tower.

# Chapter 3: Into the Other

Tom hurtled after them, trying not to fall and break his neck, and saw Woodsmoke and the woman disappear into a hole in the ground he was sure hadn't been there before. Looking around the clearing he saw no sign of Beansprout, so he threw himself into the hole after them.

For several seconds, he slid and coughed as dust rose in waves around him, then he stopped with a thump, and found himself in a tunnel. Woodsmoke was looking at him in exasperation.

"You should not have followed me!"

"I'm coming with you if Beansprout is down here. She's my cousin, and I'm not leaving without her." All thoughts of his grandfather were temporarily forgotten.

Before Woodsmoke could answer, the woman shouted, "Come on!"

Woodsmoke pulled Tom to his feet. "Stay close." He looked above Tom's head, murmuring something under his breath that Tom couldn't understand, and the entrance above disappeared, as did the faint shaft of light. Tom experienced a moment of panic as he realised he was trapped, but before he could say anything, Woodsmoke set off after the woman.

Tom followed. The tunnel was narrow and dark, lit by occasional burning torches attached to the wall, their flames giving off acrid smoke that made Tom's eyes smart. The roof was low and the walls rough, with tree roots spearing in from all directions.

Woodsmoke moved ahead with ease, gliding through the gaps. They reached an archway made of smooth, close-fitting stone, across the top of which words were carved in a strange language.

Woodsmoke shouted, "Brenna, wait!"

The woman called back, her voice flattened by the earth above them. "Hurry up!"

Beyond the arch, the tunnel walls were made of the same smooth grey stone, and the path sloped downwards, deeper into the earth.

Tom couldn't understand how the woman had got ahead of them so quickly, but as they rounded a corner, he saw her standing in the middle of a high-domed space. Brenna had the whitest skin he'd ever seen, but her hair, falling long and straight to the base of her back, was so black that it had glints of blue in it. In contrast to her skin, her eyes were dark, the whites barely visible. Like Woodsmoke, she carried a sword at her belt. She looked completely at home in this space. It seemed to fold around her.

The floor was laid with intricately carved stones forming patterns of diamonds, circles, and interlocking squares, while the walls were decorated with patterns of leaves and animals—fierce-looking winged creatures with hooves and fangs. Tom thought he could hear murmurings and rustlings.

Around the edge of the semi-circular cavern were four arched entranceways. Beyond each was a black void; it was as if the floor just dropped away. Beansprout was nowhere in sight.

"Where is she? Did you see where she went?"

Woodsmoke asked, his tone urgent.

Brenna replied calmly. "She went into the Realm of Water."

Woodsmoke turned to Tom. "You must wait here. It's too dangerous for you to come with us."

Tom looked around at this strange place so far beneath the earth, and knew he must go, too. They didn't know Beansprout—they would need his help to find her. And besides, what if something came out of those arches? What if Woodsmoke and Brenna never came back? He would die down here, entombed.

"No," he said. "I'm coming. You can bring us both back." In those seconds, Tom felt the weight of the backpack on his shoulders and tasted the decay in the air around him, and knew he was being watched by all those hundreds of eyes in the carvings as they waited with him in the long-abandoned tunnel.

Woodsmoke swore under his breath and glanced at Brenna. She nodded, and Woodsmoke muttered, "Don't say I didn't warn you!" He extended one hand to Tom and the other to Brenna. She turned and quickly pulled them into one of the archways.

For several seconds Tom felt completely weightless, and couldn't tell if he was falling, flying, or simply suspended in the dark, a speck in an ocean of blackness. He heard a murmur of sound, like waves lapping a beach, and a whispered *"Welcome,"* then felt a wrenching pull in the centre of his body. All at once there was light and ground beneath his feet. He felt himself cry out as air was forced from his body, and his hands instinctively reached out to protect himself as he pitched forward onto a mixture of hard grey rock and moss.

Taking a deep breath, he pushed back onto his haunches and looked around. They were on a broad stone path in the centre of a large, horseshoe-shaped curve of rock and water. Granite cliffs stretched high into the air, and waterfalls streamed down from the misty heights into an enormous lake in front of them, frothing and churning where they hit the water. The cliffs were pitted with caves and crevasses, and ferns grew everywhere, anchored to the rock with clinging roots. A broad stone bridge crossed to the far side of the lake, and beyond that a deep gorge disappeared into the distance.

The air was hot and very humid. Despite the fact that the sun was sinking in a cloudless, pale blue sky, the oppressive heat lay across them like a blanket, and sweat was already beading on Tom's brow.

Woodsmoke and Brenna seemed nervous, and Woodsmoke whispered, "It brought us here? To the Eye? Of all the places..."

Brenna's pallor was almost luminous in this light, which made her eyes appear even darker. She quickly checked their surroundings and seemed to come to a decision. "There's no turning back now, and at least it's not night yet. We must be quick—and quiet!"

Tom wanted to ask where they were, and what the Eye was, and who had whispered in his head so quietly it was as if he'd imagined it, but Brenna's words stilled his tongue.

They hurried to cross the bridge. It wasn't until he was halfway across it that Tom thought to look below him, into the clear green water, and he stopped, astonished. Beneath the surface was a huge castle with turrets, courtyards, and towers. It was completely intact, not a ruin that had been swallowed by the lake. Far below he saw lights flashing in the darkness on the floor of the lake, and wondered who lived there.

He ran to catch up to Woodsmoke, pulling at his arm. "There's a castle in the lake!"

Woodsmoke hissed, "*Shush*!"

Chastised, Tom continued in silence. The bridge ended with a low parapet, and they gazed over its edge. Water from the lake thundered to the base of the gorge to form a fast-flowing river. He saw a figure down there, much further along, on the right.

"Look—out there. Is that Beansprout? Why is she down there?" Tom asked, bewildered.

"The doorways open onto different spaces, depending on the time you enter," Brenna told him. "The closer you are in time when you cross, the closer in distance you will be. That's why we had to come here quickly."

"We have to get down there. She must be terrified!"

Brenna looked at Woodsmoke. "I'll go first, I can wait with her. We'll walk back this way." Then, in front of Tom's eyes, she turned into a big black bird and plunged over the edge, heading towards Beansprout.

Astonished, Tom said, "What is this place? Where am I?"

"You're in the Eye, which is the centre of The Realm of Water. It can be dangerous, so we need to leave. Stay quiet."

Woodsmoke led the way to the right, down a wide stone ramp that dropped to the floor of the gorge. The cliffs on either side were so high that Tom felt the size of an ant. It seemed to take forever to cross a small distance, as if they were crawling. It didn't help that he kept slowing down to look around him. On the opposite side of the gorge was an identical ramp; the gorge was in symmetry. He wondered who had designed it all. It was peaceful and beautiful.

"We haven't got all day, Tom. Hurry up." Woodsmoke's strides were long and fluid, and Tom almost had to jog to keep up with him.

"Is this where you live?"

"No, I live in the Realm of Earth, which is where your granddad is." Woodsmoke kept his voice low, and Tom struggled to hear him.

"Is that close? Are we going there next?"

"No. You are going home next. And keep close to the cliff side. We'll be less visible there."

Tom decided to ignore the 'going home' warning and asked, "Why is it sometimes dangerous here?"

"The water spirits who live here are not always friendly, and there are other things lurking in the rocks and the water that are even more frightening. It is not good that it's so late in the day." He looked thoughtfully at Tom and asked, "Why did your cousin go into a tunnel she doesn't know, and then enter an archway that is black and appears to lead nowhere? Is she stupid?"

It was a good question. Tom wasn't sure how to answer, but he thought he should defend Beansprout, because he was actually pleased to be here.

"She's quite inquisitive," was all he could think of.

"Really?"

Tom thought he detected sarcasm. "I suppose she thought she was helping. She probably thought our grandfather was living in the tunnel beneath the folly."

"Really?" Woodsmoke said again.

"Well, I would have thought so if I'd seen the tunnel. I probably would have done the same thing. Anyway, it's your fault. You left the tunnel open."

Woodsmoke's eyes narrowed as he stared at Tom. "Actually, Brenna did."

Tom realised he'd better not be cheeky, or Woodsmoke might leave him here.

It was nearly dark when they reached the others. Brenna and Beansprout were waiting inside a small cleft in the rock face.

"Tom!" Beansprout said nervously. "Sorry to have caused so much trouble." She looked as if she was going to hug him, but thought better of it.

"Are you okay?" he asked, relieved to see she looked in one piece.

"I am now." She smiled at Brenna. "I was a bit panic-stricken at first, but Brenna calmed me down."

"Well, this is Woodsmoke, and he's annoyed! Woodsmoke, my cousin, Beansprout."

Woodsmoke nodded briefly, but didn't waste time with pleasantries, instead turning to Brenna. "We need to get out of here. I think we should go higher, find a cave, and get out of sight."

"I've already found one." Brenna pointed to a small black hole in the rock wall, a short distance above the path. "It's small, but there are no other caves leading off it. It's the best we can do for now."

Woodsmoke sighed. "All right. Lead the way."

# Chapter 4: The Eye

Excitement and nervousness fought inside Tom's head. He wanted to see more of the Eye and the Realm of Water, but he didn't want to come across the weird and dangerous creatures that lurked beneath the waters. Well, actually he did want to see them, but from a safe distance.

The four of them were at the back of a shallow cave looking out over the gorge. It was hot and airless, and Tom was uncomfortably sweaty. He could just see Woodsmoke and Brenna in the darkness as they leaned against the walls, seemingly deep in thought.

"So what's the plan?" he asked.

"We need to find another portal, Tom," Woodsmoke said, "so we can take you back home. The portals between the four worlds are rarely used now. We certainly don't know where to find one here, so we'll need to search, but we can't do that at night." He groaned and rubbed his hands across his face. "It could take us days. And if we can't find one, it will be a long journey back to our realm."

Beansprout spoke, her voice quiet. "I'm sorry. It's my fault we're here. I got carried away…" Her voice trailed off with a sigh.

Tom asked, "What happened?"

"I'd just come out of the tower when I saw the hole in

the ground and thought I should check it out—you know, just in case. So I stuck my head in and then ended up sliding in." She shrugged. "Once I was in, I thought I'd see where it went."

"But why didn't you call me when you saw it?"

"In case it was nothing. I followed the tunnel, which was really amazing, and then I sort of stuck my hand into that black hole, and it pulled me right in!" She sounded sheepish and delighted with herself all at the same time. "I freaked out initially, kind of froze, and then decided I should sit tight and hope someone came for me—and here you are!"

Woodsmoke sounded angry. "Well, you are very lucky we found you intact. In fact, you are lucky we found you at all."

The word 'intact' seemed to hang in the air.

"I am *really* sorry," Beansprout repeated. "I know it was stupid, but it was exciting, too! It's not every day you find a hidden passage. I have food to share as an apology, if that helps?"

"Great idea," Tom answered, trying to ease her guilt. "I'll share mine, too. While we eat you can tell us about this place, and how you know our granddad."

"Very well," Woodsmoke said, and while Beansprout and Tom passed out food, he began. "First, you need to know we are no longer in your world. I'm sure that's obvious. We are in the Otherworld, which lies alongside yours. There are four realms here—Earth, Air, Water and Fire—and different spirits and beings live in each. This, as you know, is the Realm of Water, and we have arrived in the Eye, the absolute centre of the realm, where the Emperor lives. Brenna and I are from the Realm of Earth. Years ago we passed between the four realms all the time, but for years now we have remained separate. It's the same with your world—we no longer come and go from there as we used to. In your world we have different names—faeries, elves, fauns, nymphs, or even Sidhe."

"Faeries!" gasped Beansprout. "Like in the old stories—the ones where people would disappear and never be seen again?"

"That's right. At certain times of day—dawn and dusk—and in certain places, the boundaries between our worlds would dissolve and humans could pass from their world to ours, usually by accident. Now, for most people, only the portals will enable passage, but they're well hidden."

"Hidden how? By magic?" asked Tom.

"Of a sort. And they are usually built underground, or in remote places, with concealed entrances. My grandfather, Fahey, was trapped in your world for many years. When he was released from the spell, he managed to find the portals in the wood. He said he could hear our realm singing to him, as if to call him home, and he followed the music."

Beansprout paused, her sandwich halfway to her mouth. "Where was he trapped?"

"In that old yew tree at the edge of the wood beyond Jack's garden. He was trying to travel to Avalon, but triggered a spell. For years we had no idea what had happened to him, although we searched and searched." Woodsmoke shook his head at the memory. "And then he returned a few moons ago with your grandfather, who was the first person he saw after he was released from the spell."

"Wow! Your grandfather was trapped in a tree!" Tom exclaimed, "So why is Granddad here?"

"My grandfather asked him to join him, and I guess he liked the offer. I know how much I missed my grandfather—

that's why I agreed to bring you that package, so you wouldn't worry."

Tom nodded as he listened, happy to finally have some answers. "So *your* grandfather, Fahey, is *our* grandfather's new friend."

"No wonder he was so vague," Beansprout pointed out. "He couldn't have told the truth! We would have thought he'd gone senile."

"Then you must know why we want to see him, Woodsmoke," Tom persisted.

Woodsmoke shuffled uncomfortably. "I do, but it's not that easy. Our world is dangerous, full of magic, strange places and even stranger creatures. It's far more dangerous than your world is to us. I have heard rumours of the Emperor here. If they are true, he's someone we should keep away from."

"If this is the Realm of Water, why are we on land?" Beansprout asked.

"A portion of it is land, although it's filled with rivers and waterways. Most of the realm is under the sea. Whole cities are sprawled across the sea bed, or perched on underwater mountain ranges or deep within trenches, far from light. From what I have heard there are different groups there who all fight for control, and petty skirmishes are constantly breaking out. The Emperor must be a busy man," Woodsmoke said thoughtfully.

"Do people fight in the Realm of Earth, too?" Tom asked.

"Sometimes. There are disturbing rumours coming out of the Aeriken Forest in our realm. The Queen of the Aerikeen is strange, and rarely seen. Her people have disappeared from the villages." He exchanged a worried glance with Brenna. "We fear something terrible is happening there."

"Do you know Jack too, Brenna?" Beansprout asked.

"Yes," she answered from the darkness. "At the moment, I live with Woodsmoke and his family. We're friends. I said I would travel with him, for safety. And I was curious, too. After meeting Jack, I wanted to know what your world was like."

Tom was still determined to try to find him. "If Granddad's safe, then it must be all right here."

"Your grandfather is with Fahey, in a safe area," Woodsmoke replied. "We are a long way from there."

While they were talking, there was an almighty roaring sound, and the clatter of what sounded like hooves racing along the path. Shouting started to fill the gorge.

"By Herne's horns!" Woodsmoke sounded exasperated, and he jumped to his feet and peered out of the cave. "I think we've been found," he said over his shoulder.

Tom's heart beat faster, as if it might leap out of his chest. Beansprout waited motionless beside him. The rumbling and clattering became louder, accompanied by wild singing and laughing. A huge, towering water spout erupted from the river, filling the cave with spray, before collapsing and leaving a murky green light to illuminate the night.

Woodsmoke stepped back as a large figure appeared in the cave entrance, a black shadow against the eerie green glow. A booming voice declared, "Welcome to the Eye, travellers." It didn't sound welcoming.

Woodsmoke replied with a bow, "Greetings, we thank you for your welcome."

The voice answered, "The Emperor is waiting to see you." He stepped aside, gesturing for them to leave.

He left them no choice, and as they made their way out of the cave, they saw dozens of horses below them, carrying men and women armed with swords and spears. The green light was coming from the middle of the river, and it illuminated a mass of giant tentacles that seemed to be reaching for them.

They scrambled down to the path, and were each hustled onto a horse with another rider. The animals stamped impatiently until the four of them were seated, then wheeled around, heading back to the lake. Tom gripped his rider anxiously. He'd never been on a horse before, and was convinced he was going to be thrown off.

The castle that had been beneath the water was now above it, with hundreds of lights shining from the windows. They raced up the broad ramp, along the parapet, and onto the bridge that had previously crossed the lake, but which now led to huge gates in the castle walls. They swept through them and entered a courtyard that felt like a prison. Its sheer black granite walls rose above them, and Tom glanced nervously around, noting Beansprout's worried face. He tried to smile reassuringly, but failed. The riders quickly dismounted, and tossed the reins to others who emerged from the shadows, before heading towards a broad entrance on the left.

Tom, Beansprout, Woodsmoke, and Brenna waited in silence, wondering where they were expected to go. Tom imagined deep, dark dungeons, dank and cold. However, the man with the booming voice shepherded them into a large dining hall, crowded with people eating and drinking at long tables. Servants milled around, replenishing enormous plates and dishes as the sound of music came from a group in the corner of the room.

The room fell silent as everyone turned to look at them.

A voice came from the far end of the room. "So, our visitors *finally* arrive in my hall."

Craning his neck, Tom saw a man, his dark hair streaked with grey, sitting at a table raised on a dais. He leaned forward on his ornate chair, looking at them intently. This must be the Emperor.

Woodsmoke and Brenna immediately bowed, a sweeping gesture reaching down to their feet, and Woodsmoke said, "I would like to apologise for our unannounced presence in the Eye. It was completely unplanned, and we were aiming to be out before disturbing Your Majesty."

"Were you indeed?" The Emperor's voice boomed out across the hall. "And what did you hope to achieve by visiting the Eye? Are you spies?"

"No! We came to rescue this human child who passed through the portal. It was an accident."

Tom felt all eyes fall on him and his cousin. He opened his mouth to take the blame, but before he could speak, Beansprout said in a shaky voice, "I'm sorry, Your Majesty. It was my fault. I didn't realise what would happen."

"So, human child, it is you who brings visitors to my hall." The Emperor peered closely at them. "How did you find the doorway? It has surely been closed for many years."

"I saw a hole in the ground and found it that way."

"It was our fault," interrupted Woodsmoke. "We left the passage open. But I would like to reassure you that it is now closed, and with Your Majesty's permission, we will leave tomorrow to return the visitors to their home. If you could direct us to a portal, it would be most helpful."

"And what," asked the Emperor, "are two of the fey from the Realm of Earth doing with humans? Didn't we stop passing to their world many hundreds of years ago?"

"I had to deliver a message. A guest came to our realm of late. He wanted to send a message to his family, telling them that he was safe."

The Emperor paused, his face stern as he stared at Woodsmoke. He spoke softly. "It has also been a very long time since anyone from the Realm of Earth came to the Eye."

Woodsmoke gave a thin smile. "Too long. But you are not who we expected to see, Your Majesty."

After another long pause, during which there was only a breathless silence, the Emperor said, "No, I would not be. There have been many changes here." He gazed into the middle distance for a moment, and suddenly relaxed. "Well, I would be a poor host if I did not offer you food. Come and sit, all of you, and you can tell me what is happening in your realms."

With that, the general hum of noise started again. The people sitting around the Emperor moved aside to make room, and Tom and Beansprout sat on the Emperor's left, while Woodsmoke and Brenna sat to his right. The Emperor started talking to Woodsmoke, leaving Tom and Beansprout to entertain themselves.

Servants put plates in front of them, and they picked from the platters in the centre of the table. There were whole baked fish the length of a man's body, piles of mussels and oysters, and steaming bowls of fish stew. Tom took a bite of something green that was probably fried seaweed, and discretely spat it into a table napkin. Beansprout was merrily tucking into a huge bowl of trifle.

Looking around the room, Tom realised the other guests weren't really 'people,' in the usual sense of the word. Neither were Woodsmoke and Brenna. The Emperor had called them 'fey.' Tom couldn't quite explain what made them different, other than a peculiar awareness they seemed to have. It was quite unnerving. When they looked at you, it was as if they could see right into your mind. Not to mention, Brenna could turn into a bird! He wondered if the people in the Eye could turn into animals, too. They looked a little different from Woodsmoke and Brenna. Their skin was slightly shimmery, as if dusted with silver, and their eyes were a bright, shiny blue. And the castle—what an amazing place! This hall was similar to the old English halls he'd seen in books, but instead of having fireplaces, there were fountains in alcoves along the wall. The water seemed to cool the hall, a welcome change from the sticky heat outside.

Tom tried to look at the Emperor without being too obvious about it, watching him out of the corner of his eye. He was much younger than Tom had thought an Emperor would be. His hair was pulled up into a knot on his head, his face was sharp, his eyebrows high and quizzical, and he wore long, loose robes of dark blue, which pooled like water at his feet. His chair looked as if it were made from polished coral.

Suddenly, Tom felt a long way from home. It was hard to believe that only this morning they were in the wood by his house. It was then that Tom realised his father would have no idea where he was, or Beansprout's family, but there was nothing he could do now. He still wanted to see his granddad before going back.

Tom was incredibly tired, and he noticed Beansprout's eyes beginning to close, her head nodding gently before she snapped it up, trying to stay awake. He turned to her. "You okay?"

"Exhausted. But I don't want to go to bed—there's too

much to see. This is all so weird." She shook her head as she gazed at their surroundings.

"I know exactly what you mean. Do you still want to find Granddad?"

"Absolutely! We're so close, it would be mad not to. Woodsmoke will take us. We'll make him!"

"Good, because I'm not ready to go home yet." He gestured at the room. "This place was under water earlier. Can you believe that? And nothing is wet. Well, not like you'd expect."

Beansprout stared at him, wide-eyed, trying to stifle a yawn. "Really? How does that happen? We have to stay. Have to!"

The Emperor turned their way, saw Beansprout yawning, and immediately summoned a servant. "Give our guests a room each in the East Tower." Turning back to them, he said, "You two are tired. You do not keep such late hours as we do. Sleep now, and we will talk tomorrow."

Tom caught Woodsmoke's attention, and he nodded reassuringly, so they followed the servant out of the hall.

He led them along winding corridors and up stairs both grand and sweeping and small and spiralling, until they were completely disorientated. They ended up on a short corridor and were shown rooms next to each other. Tom lay on his bed thinking he'd be awake all night, but in minutes he was fast asleep.

# Chapter 5: The Dectopus

Several hours later, Tom woke up feeling groggy and disorientated, and for a few seconds, couldn't work out where he was.

As the events from the previous day began to filter into his thoughts, his confusion vanished and he shot up in bed, looking around wildly. Then, he remembered—he was in the bedroom in the tower. Flopping back down, he wondered if this was what jetlag felt like.

His dreams started to return to him. Again, the white-haired woman had appeared, but this time the image had been sharper, clearer. She'd looked impatient, saying, *"Come, Tom, you are nearly here. Hurry! There are things you must do."* Firelight overtook his vision, and he'd felt its heat as chanting filled his ears. She was infuriating.

With a shock, Tom realised it had been her voice he had heard when they crossed through the portal. Who was she? *What things must he do?*

Tom sighed as he sat up again, knowing he could no longer ignore her messages. They meant something. He looked around, wondering why the room was filled with a dull green light. Were there leaves over the window? Then he had another thought. He jumped out of bed, ran to the window, and whistled under his breath.

They were surrounded by water.

Large, tree-like plants waved about in the current, their thick, knotted roots anchored into the rock. Fish of all sizes swam past the window, and horses grazed on the lake floor. Looking up, he saw a pale yellow disc, and the surface of the lake glinting like a mirror far above. Shafts of sunlight pierced the gloom.

The urge to explore woke Tom fully. On a table in the corner of his room was a bowl of steaming water, a bar of soap, and towels. He had a quick wash and raked his fingers through his hair, and then dragged his clothes on, noting they were freshly laundered. Wondering if Beansprout was awake, he stepped into the empty corridor and knocked on her door.

She shouted, "Come in!" She was at the window, staring into the water. "Tom! You were right, the castle is under the water! How is this possible?"

"Magic, I guess."

"But how do we get out of here? We're trapped."

"I'm more worried about how we find breakfast! Fancy a wander?"

"Should we? What if we get lost?"

"Oh, we'll definitely get lost, but we're lost anyway, aren't we?" He shrugged and smiled.

Grabbing their packs, they headed down the corridor, attempting to retrace their steps from the night before. They met no one, and the castle was eerily silent. Before long, it was clear they were lost; the ornate hallways were different to those they had walked along the night before. The walls were hung with tapestries of underwater scenes, and decorated with the skeletal remains of unfamiliar creatures. Rills of water trickled down the edges of the corridors, and there were small pools filled with lily pads and plants that they didn't recognise.

"I think we're in the main part of the castle, Tom," Beansprout whispered.

They had come to a large, circular space with a grand staircase leading down to an atrium. Huge windows let in the green glow of the water, and large, purple fronds of aquatic plants tapped against the panes.

"Let's head down," Tom said, leading the way, and as they reached the bottom, a door opened on the far side of the room and a woman stepped out.

She looked surprised for the briefest of seconds, and then smiled. "You must be our human visitors. Follow me."

On the far side of the atrium, a wooden arched doorway led to a courtyard, and she ushered them through it. Above them, water was suspended from its downward rush by some mysterious force.

"Don't worry," the Emperor called. "It's quite safe." He was seated at a stone table laden with food and what looked like a pot of tea. "Come and join me, I have much to ask you."

With a nervous glance at each other and at the water overhead, Tom and Beansprout headed to the table. They sat while the Emperor poured tea—which was most definitely not normal tea—and offered them fish for breakfast. Tom took a sip of the green liquid and tried not to grimace; it was an odd-tasting, salty brew.

"Woodsmoke has been telling me how you came to be here. I trust you are enjoying yourselves?"

Tom answered for them, trying to swallow his food quickly. "Yes. It's…different."

"Years ago," the Emperor began, "many people from your world visited here—accidentally, of course—but it was easier then. The doorways were simpler to find and the walls between our worlds came and went. Only those who know where to look visit now, but few have this knowledge. Those who do come are not always friendly." He looked regretful. "It has also been a long time since we saw anyone from the Realm of Earth. As I explained to your friends last night, I have been Emperor since my father died, and things have been difficult. My father was suspicious, and treated visitors badly. I understand why your friends were worried about being here. He would probably have fed you to the Mantis."

Beansprout's face grew pale.

"We have tried to keep my father's death a secret. This has allowed me to make changes and defeat certain groups, particularly the swamp goblins." Noticing Beansprout's discomfort, he changed the subject, smiling brightly. "Tell me all about you. I once visited your world, when the forests ran thick, tangled, and unbroken right to the shores of your seas. What is it like now?"

Between them they attempted to answer his question, and were on to their third pot of so-called tea when Woodsmoke and Brenna appeared, looking more relaxed than the day before, and not in the slightest concerned at the water suspended high above their heads. They joined them at the table, and the Emperor gestured that they should help themselves to breakfast.

The Emperor addressed Woodsmoke. "Last night, I agreed to escort you to our closest portal to the Realm of Earth. Unfortunately, my father destroyed many portals, particularly those to your world," he said, looking at Tom and Beansprout, "so I cannot send you directly home. But I think you are not displeased with that?" He looked amused at their excited faces.

Tom straightened his shoulders. "We still want to find our grandfather."

Brenna suppressed a smile as Woodsmoke rolled his eyes, but the Emperor continued. "The remaining portals are deep underground, and we need to travel along a river to get there. But," he hesitated, concerned. "It's not the easiest trip, or the safest place to be. Instead, I suggest that we escort you up the river that runs to the border. However, that too will be a difficult journey, passing through swamps and then the mangrove forests, which, at this time of year, are full of flesh flies, and it could take many weeks—"

Woodsmoke shook his head, interrupting. "No. That would take far too long. We have to attempt the portal."

"Very well, then. We shall leave tonight." He rose to his feet. "I must go, affairs of state demand my attention. Feel free to explore the castle. Your rooms are at your disposal, and I shall ensure this table remains stocked with food for you."

Once he'd left, Beansprout said, "Please let us stay with you! We're so close to seeing Granddad!"

"I don't think we have much choice," Brenna said, sighing. "You heard him. The portal to your world is closed, so we have to return to our realm to get there. But, we have no idea where we may find ourselves. It's not that we are trying to be mean … it's just that our world is dangerous. Woodsmoke wasn't lying yesterday. We're just thinking of your safety."

"But if we go back to our world now, we'll never see him again," Tom pointed out. "Unless you think Granddad will return home?"

Woodsmoke rubbed his chin thoughtfully as he met Brenna's gaze across the table. "I don't think that will happen. Not for a long time, anyway." His shoulders sagged as he came to a decision. "All right, we'll see what we can do. In the meantime, I think we should accept the Emperor's gracious offer and explore this place. I doubt very much if any of us will ever return here again."

For the rest of the day, they roamed the castle, exploring endless halls, a ballroom, elegant sitting rooms, and bedrooms. They eventually found their way to the dungeons, where they were politely shown around a small part before being ushered away, the sound of wailing following them up the corridor. They all decided to get a few hours of sleep in the late afternoon, when they finally found their rooms again, and then met in the courtyard for food.

After the sun had set, and the water around them had become black and impenetrable, the castle rose majestically to the surface of the lake. It was a discomforting experience to find themselves shooting upwards, the floor rocking beneath them as if there was an earthquake. The roar of water filled the castle, and Tom felt his ears become thick with pressure, all sound becoming muffled, before they popped and everything returned to normal. The bubble around the courtyard that had kept the water suspended disappeared, and the warm night's breeze rolled over them.

Tom released his grip on the table. "Well, that was different!"

Woodsmoke laughed. "It's an interesting place, isn't it?"

"That's one word for it."

Beansprout started giggling, which set them all off, and they were still laughing when one of the courtiers came to fetch them. He escorted them to the rear gates of the castle, where the Emperor was waiting with a dozen men carrying lanterns. The gates swung open and they stepped onto the stone bridge, but this time headed towards the granite cliffs and the thundering waterfalls, pausing at the rocky ledge.

"We'll summon the hippocamps," the Emperor told them.

"Sea horses," said Woodsmoke, in response to Tom's baffled expression.

One of the Emperor's men pulled a flute out of his pocket and blew into it, and just moments later, four horses broke the surface, whinnying softly as they swam towards the shore. They had normal horse heads, but the manes trailing down their backs were webbed and transparent. Small wings sprouted from their sides, and large fishtails propelled them through the water.

Beansprout leaned forward to pat them. "They're so beautiful!"

"Oh yes, and quite tame," the Emperor said, looking at them affectionately. "We use them to pull our boats. You'll see."

He nodded to one of the men, who turned and led the way to one side of the waterfall, pushing through lush ferns into a partially hidden cleft in the rock. They followed him down a passageway that eventually led to a fast-flowing river. In one direction, the river joined the lake; in the other, it disappeared into darkness.

A boat was moored up, and the hippocamps were waiting next to it. There were no sails; instead Tom saw neatly stacked oars alongside rows of seats. The men harnessed the animals to the front before boarding the vessel, hanging their lanterns along the sides and on the prow. Tom, Beansprout, Woodsmoke, and Brenna made their way to the stern with the Emperor. When everyone was seated, they gently pushed out.

The air in the tunnel was damp, and the walls trickled with water. Beansprout shivered. Woodsmoke offered her his cloak, and she wrapped it around her shoulders, throwing him a grateful smile. Beyond the ship the darkness was absolute, but their progress was slow and steady.

The Emperor turned to them, frowning. "We have had much rain lately so the river should be deep enough to take us all the way to the portal. In some places the current is swift and strong, so don't fall in."

"How far does the river go?" asked Tom.

"Oh, miles and miles—far beyond our destination. But it eventually becomes narrower, and then you have to climb. There are many waterfalls, and places where the water completely fills the caverns. The traveller must take great care to avoid those. And the river branches off in many places. It is easy to become lost. Some have entered here and never been seen again." He paused, then added, "You're lucky the portal didn't bring you here when you arrived." His words hung in the air and seemed to echo in the enclosed space.

Tom felt a cold shudder run down his spine as he realised they could have emerged anywhere. "Could we have ended up in the sea?"

"Oh yes, the portals can be quite hazardous."

Understatement of the year. Tom turned to Woodsmoke and Brenna. "Could we come out somewhere really dangerous in your realm?"

Brenna nodded. "Yes, but we know our world well, so hopefully we'll be fine. We may still have further to travel than we would want, though."

Woodsmoke added a word of warning. "This place is not for the unprepared traveller. Like your own world, ours has areas that are hostile to outsiders."

"Blimey," said Beansprout, retreating into the cloak with another shudder. "I wish I'd known that before I stuck my hand in."

Tom couldn't relax; there was too much to see. He examined the boat, noting that it looked familiar, and for a second, he couldn't work out why. Then it struck him, and he turned to the Emperor, excited. "This boat reminds me of the Greek ships I've seen in history books."

"Ah, how clever of you, Tom! It is in fact a version of the trireme, one of the ships we introduced to the Greeks. We were very influential in the Mediterranean many years ago. We are a seafaring people—"

"Really?" he interrupted, disbelief in his voice. "You helped the Greeks?"

"Oh, only slightly," the Emperor answered modestly. "Not me, personally—I was far too young. Unfortunately, we are also responsible for the presence of the giant squid and sea serpents in your seas. An accidental crossing from our world."

Tom now had so many questions whizzing around his head, he didn't know which to ask first. "Sea serpents? But they're a myth. And how old are you? That was over two thousand years ago!"

The Emperor looked at the floor and scratched his chin. "Well, I am older than I look. We are a race that lives for many years. Woodsmoke and Brenna are much older than you imagine, as well."

Beansprout, who had been following the conversation with some interest, butted in. "So how old are you two?"

Woodsmoke laughed. "I am four hundred and twenty-three years old—quite young, really. What about you, Brenna?"

"Oh, three hundred and seventy, or thereabouts," she said with a wry smile.

Tom and Beansprout looked at each in shock, but the Emperor was already continuing, oblivious to the bombshell he'd just dropped.

"If you're interested in sea creatures, Tom, we may see one later. Or perhaps you're not that interested," he added, noting Tom's wary expression.

"Where might we see one?" Tom asked nervously.

"We are going to the Cavern of the Four Portals—although there are of course only three now. It's a huge cave, and this river flows into it, forming a deep lake that is connected to the sea by a long underground river. Its current is quite treacherous. One of our greatest explorers found it. Unfortunately, on occasions a giant dectopus swims up the passageway and takes up residence in the lake. If it's there, we must try not to disturb it." He looked at their worried faces and added, "I'm sure we won't."

Tom glanced nervously at Beansprout and asked, "What's a dectopus?"

"It is a ten-tentacled sea creature. Haven't you heard of them?"

"I've only heard of an octopus."

"Well, there you are, then. Much the same, just a bit bigger." He shrugged nonchalantly, as if it was the most ordinary thing in the world.

Tom nodded, murmuring, "Oh, of course."

He noticed Woodsmoke and Brenna exchange worried glances, and Beansprout pulled the cloak even further up to her chin. They fell silent, listening to the sound of the hippocamps splashing in the inky black river. At least, Tom hoped it was the hippocamps.

They had been travelling a while when the river started to curl to the left and the passageway became bigger. The torchlight showed the rock walls were slick with moisture, and stalactites hung from the roof, streaks of pink and yellow glimmering like underground rainbows. Tom became more and more aware of the huge amount of rock over their heads as they moved still further underground. Tributaries opened up on either side, and water poured down from the suffocating blackness, carrying the sound of strange gurgles and splashes. Every now and again the Emperor would impart some bit of knowledge about the warren of tunnels and mysterious whirlpools they were passing, but their worried faces eventually drove him to silence.

Just as Tom was beginning to think the journey would never end, the passage opened up, and Tom realised they were at the entrance to the cavern the Emperor had mentioned. He leaned forward, eager to see more. One of the rowers touched the wick from his lantern to the wall, and a band of bright orange flame raced along the rock face. He did the same on the other side of the passage, and the cavern became brighter as the flames spread in a circle beneath a domed roof. Craning his neck, Tom saw huge, elaborate carvings on the walls towering above him, depicting fights between enormous sea creatures. They seemed to move in the flickering light, and Tom's mouth dropped open with wonder.

On the far side of the lake was a long narrow pier, beyond which was a broad stone floor on which boxes and ropes were coiled. Behind the boxes, rough stone steps led to a dark, shadowy recess. They had reached the portals.

As soon as they had enough room around the boat, the men reached for their oars and started to pull, assisting the hippocamps to pull the boat across the lake.

Tom turned to the Emperor. "What are all the boxes for?"

"This is where we built the boat, so there are building materials for repairs, and we store other things here, for journeying further inland." He nodded to the rear of the cavern where the river exited into another tunnel.

As they passed the centre of the pool, bubbles appeared on the surface. The hippocamps became nervous, snorting wildly and straining towards the shore. Seeing the commotion, two men in the prow raised their short sharpened tridents and stood, peering into the water.

"Is it the dectopus?" Beansprout asked, looking alarmed.

No one answered, but they all rose to their feet. Woodsmoke raised his longbow, keeping his eyes on the water, and Brenna pulled her sword free from its scabbard.

The Emperor touched Tom and Beansprout gently on the arm, pulling them back from the side of the ship. "Stay in the middle."

The hippocamps pulled furiously towards the shore, and the rowers doubled their efforts, their combining strength making them lurch forward, and Tom stumbled. Then, in front of them, a sleek and scaly tentacle uncoiled on the surface before plunging into the depths again. For a few seconds, the water fell still, and then several more tentacles appeared, followed by the enormous, bulbous body of the dectopus. It reared into the air, water streaming over it. Its skin was wrinkled and thick like an elephant's, and two enormous eyes blinked slowly. It flicked several tentacles towards them, and Tom saw its suckers raised and ready to grasp the ship.

Beansprout screamed. Woodsmoke released several

arrows at its head. Some found their target, but most bounced off into the water. Before Woodsmoke could shoot again, the dectopus plunged back beneath the surface, making the boat rock wildly.

"He wasn't kidding when he said giant dectopus!" Tom exclaimed.

The boat raced onwards, but the dectopus rose again, this time on their starboard side. Another volley of arrows left Woodsmoke's bow, but again the dectopus's tentacles whipped across the surface of the pool. One grabbed a hippocamp, ripping it free of its harness and dropping it into its gaping mouth. Other tentacles latched onto the ship, causing it to rock wildly. Everyone grabbed for something fixed; Tom slid across the deck and hit the side, hurting his elbow. Brenna rolled and quickly regained her feet, slashing at the closest tentacle. The dectopus roared in pain, the noise echoing around the cave, but the ship tipped further. Woodsmoke and the Emperor withdrew their swords and joined Brenna's attack, and they slashed at the tentacles as the men released a volley of tridents. With another roar the dectopus finally released the ship, and it shot upright, waves rolling across the deck.

The remaining hippocamps had broken free and were racing away with deafening shrieks that echoed around the cave, before they disappeared beneath the surface of the water.

"Keep rowing!" the Emperor yelled at his men, and other than a few who remained poised with their tridents, the rest pulled on the oars.

They were within reach of the pier when the dectopus emerged directly ahead. It towered above them, and this time its tentacles grabbed both sides of the boat, pulling it towards its open mouth. A tentacle whipped across their heads, its huge suckers flexing, and it grabbed one of the Emperor's men. With a scream, he was dropped into its gaping jaw.

"Abandon ship!" commanded the Emperor, as they were dragged ever closer to the giant creature.

Tom grabbed Beansprout and pushed her forward. "Go!" he shouted.

They jumped into the churning water together, Tom gasping as he hit the icy lake. It was so cold it felt like a fist was squeezing his lungs. The water blinded and deafened him, and he flailed around, desperately trying to reach the surface, but his clothes dragged him down. His head finally emerged, and he gasped for air.

Tom found himself surrounded by seething water and thrashing tentacles. Were there only ten? It seemed like so many more. He heard an enormous, splintering crack, and watched as a chunk of the boat was ripped off and sent flying overhead, and he started swimming for the shore. A hippocamp appeared beneath him, and he grasped its webbed mane as it raced across the lake, tipping him off in the shallows.

Tom staggered to dry land, then quickly ducked and rolled as a tentacle whipped towards him, missing him by inches. He saw Beansprout lying exhausted nearby and dragged her to her feet, yelling, "Run!" Together they raced for the back of the cave, and hoping they were clear of danger, turned to search the water for signs of their companions.

Woodsmoke and Brenna had also jumped out of the boat, and they watched the hippocamps deposit them on dry land a short distance away, but it seemed the Emperor's men didn't need help. They were strong swimmers, and made their own way to the shore, except for an unlucky few that were plucked from the water by the dectopus.

Woodsmoke took up position at the end of the pier, firing a blur of arrows, while Brenna helped gather a pile of silvery-looking ropes. The men separated, some clambering up the walls to where several large pieces of machinery hung high on the rocky face. Thick ropes ran from these to a giant web suspended over the pool.

The Emperor was nowhere in sight, and Tom watched the lake anxiously. The dectopus had also disappeared, abandoning the damaged boat. For several seconds nothing happened, and the water became smooth and still.

Just as Tom began to worry that the Emperor had drowned, he surfaced right under the web, the dectopus rearing next to him, and shouted, "Now!"

The giant web dropped, along with several hundredweight of stone it had supported. An enormous boom rang out as the weight crashed down onto the creature, and it sank below the surface. A large wave rose and raced to the shore, and with it came the Emperor.

"Quickly," he shouted. "Secure it with the ropes!"

His remaining men dived back into the water, dragging the ropes behind them. They were submerged for a long time.

Tom and Beansprout edged forward, fascinated by the fight, and Brenna and Woodsmoke joined them.

"How can they stay underwater for so long?" asked Beansprout.

"They're water spirits," Woodsmoke told her. "That's why their skin is silvery, almost as if they are half fish. They can swim underwater for hours. They just don't live in it."

"And what was the web thing under the roof?"

"Giant water spiders make very strong webs!"

Beansprout looked a little sick. "I hope we don't meet one of those, too."

While the Emperor and his men finished securing the dectopus, Woodsmoke lit a fire from the woodpile he found in a dry corner. They warmed themselves by the bright flames, still shocked by the violent encounter.

Woodsmoke had wrung his cloak out and place it over a wooden crate, and now he held his hands to the fire. "That was too close for comfort."

"And too close for some of the men," Brenna said sadly. "The dectopus was too quick."

"And it killed a hippocamp," Beansprout added.

"I take it you've seen the portals?" Woodsmoke gestured to the shadowy recess above them.

Tom nodded. "I suppose we'll leave when the Emperor gets back?"

"Yes. We're lucky he was feeling generous. We would never have found this place without him."

"Who built them?"

"They were built thousands of years ago, by the powerful magic of the ancient Gods."

"Oh." That wasn't the answer Tom had expected. "Which Gods?"

Woodsmoke laughed. "That tale's for another time."

The Emperor and his men finally emerged from the deep, cold waters and shook the moisture off their skin like otters.

"All done," said the Emperor with a faint smile. "We have wrapped it up so tightly, it will take weeks to break free, if it ever does. And now I'm starved. Time for food."

He joined them, while his men brought a dozen large,

rainbow-scaled fish from the half-ruined boat, lit a second fire, and spread the fish on flat grills to cook. Water and wine were handed out, and they sat talking while the smell of cooking filled the air.

"I'm sorry you've lost men," Woodsmoke said. "I feel it's our fault. It wouldn't have happened if you hadn't brought us here. We owe you a huge debt."

The Emperor sipped his wine with obvious pleasure. "Not at all. It has happened before, and will no doubt happen again. We risk these encounters all the time when we travel, and although it's sad to lose men, we accept it. I'm tempted to pass through the portal with you, but the realm remains unsettled, and I still have much to do here. Another time."

He paused to rummage in his pockets, and pulled out a curious spiral shell inlaid with silver and jade. Muttering a few words, he passed his hand across it, and then presented it to Beansprout and Tom. "A present, to remember your time in the Eye. Any time you need help and there's water nearby, just throw it in. I won't tell you what will happen. It will be a surprise. Which of you would like to look after it?"

"Thank you. Tom should," Beansprout offered immediately.

"Thanks," said Tom, hoping he wouldn't lose it as he slipped it into his pocket.

After eating, they said their goodbyes, gathered their things, and walked up the stone steps to the three portals above the lake. At the far end was a mass of rubble where the fourth had once stood. Tom wouldn't have thought it possible to destroy these doorways; they looked as if they would stand forever.

The portal to the Realm of Earth was in the middle, surrounded by carvings of trees, mountains, and strange, hoof-footed half-men. At the centre of the arch were carvings of a woman with a serene face, and a man with enormous antlers rising from his head.

Woodsmoke looked at them. "Ready?"

They nodded, and holding hands, stepped into the inky blackness and out of the Realm of Water.

# Chapter 6: In the Greenwood

With a swooping, falling motion, Tom felt the blackness slide by and heard fluttering, just for a moment, until they landed with a *thump*. This time he felt soft earth beneath his hands. He stood on shaking legs, and looking around saw they were on slope surrounded by a dense pine forest, mist curling across the ground.

Brenna stood too, her sword already drawn, and she turned slowly. "I think we're on the hills beyond the river. I recognise the woods."

Woodsmoke nodded. "It's dawn, too. That was a long night, and it's going to be a long day. Let's go."

He led them downhill, the thick carpet of pine needles swallowing their footsteps. The mist thickened and swirled around their legs in whispery tendrils, rising almost unnoticed, until the others disappeared from Tom's view. Distracted by his new surroundings, he wandered down a tunnel that hollowed out in the mist before him, finally emerging into a clearing filled with the sweet, pungent scent of honeysuckle.

A woman sat cross-legged in the centre. She was beautiful, with long white hair framing her pale face, and she seemed at once both very young and very old. Her eyes were light blue, and she wore a long grey dress edged with embroidery. With a shock, Tom realised she was the woman he had seen in his dreams.

She gazed at him, and speaking softly, said, "Tom, at last you have arrived. Come and sit so we can talk."

Trapped within the circle of mist, he warily moved closer, reluctantly sitting a short distance away.

She smiled. "I have called you here because there is something you must do."

"I think you're confusing me with someone else," he said. "I came here to find my grandfather and take him home. Who are you? How do you know my name, and how did you get into my dreams?"

"But Tom," she said, ignoring his questions. "What if he does not wish to return home?"

"Of course he does, why wouldn't he?" Tom felt a slight panic as he answered; a sense of unease as other possibilities suggested themselves.

Ignoring his question again, she said, "There is something I want you to do while you are here."

The woman was as exasperating in person as she was in his dreams. "What could you possibly want me to do?"

"I need you to wake the King who lies sleeping on the Isle of Avalon. Your friend's grandfather, Fahey, once tried to wake the King, many years ago, but it wasn't time and I sent him far from here. However, Queen Gavina has become dangerous. She hunts her own people, the Aerikeen. This is the time to wake the King, and you are the one who must wake him."

Tom sat there, dumbfounded. "What king? On where? How can I wake him if this Fahey, or whatever his name is, couldn't?"

"Because you have something Fahey didn't."

The woman held out a supple, fresh, living twig, ripe with spring growth.

"This will enable you to wake the King. Only with the bough can you do it."

Tom felt panic building in him again. "But how? I don't know where this place is. What king? Why me? And who are you?"

There was a hint of impatience in her tone. "Ask Woodsmoke. He can show you the way. It is important, Tom. The Queen's people need your help. You are linked to the King by your blood, and only someone of his own blood can wake him. And you must hurry. You have taken far too long to get here."

*Too long? What was she talking about?* Tom felt a weight in his lap and, looking down, saw that the twig had magically appeared there, and had turned from a living branch to solid silver. He picked it up, wondering how she had managed such a clever trick. Before he could ask anything else, the woman seemed to fill with light, until she was so bright that Tom had to close his eyes and cover them with his hands. When the light faded, she had gone, and he was sitting alone in bright sunshine.

The distant shouts of his friends shocked him out of his dazed state, and he called, "I'm over here!"

A large, black, glossy-plumed bird burst into the clearing and spotting him, swooped off again. It was Brenna, gone to guide the others, and within minutes they crowded around him. Beansprout appeared exasperated. "Tom, where have you been? We've been calling for hours!"

"I've been right here!" he answered crossly.

Brenna turned to Woodsmoke. "I swear I flew over here earlier, but I couldn't see him!"

Woodsmoke asked, "Are you okay? You look odd."

"I've had a weird encounter."

"What do you mean? With whom?"

"A really old woman with long white hair, dressed in grey. Except, she didn't seem old. Not really. And she had magical powers."

Brenna and Woodsmoke stood gaping at Tom, but Brenna gathered herself first. "You met the Lady of the Lake?"

Tom was bewildered. "I don't know. Did I?"

Brenna narrowed her eyes. "What did she want?"

"She said I have to wake the King."

Woodsmoke groaned and flopped backwards onto the earth, staring up at the sky. Brenna sat slowly, looking shocked, and Tom looked at Beansprout. "I have no idea what's happening!"

"Or me!" Beansprout answered, looking perplexed. She put her hands on her hips in a gesture that reminded Tom of his aunt, and he supressed a grin. "Will you two please tell us what's going on? Who's the King that Tom has to wake? Why is he asleep?"

Tom and Beansprout were still standing and Brenna squinted up at them. "Sit down. This will take a while." She waited until they were settled and then said, "Years ago, there was a famous King. He was much loved, and saved the ancient Britons from attack many times. He was given a magical sword, and he had the help of a powerful wizard. Does this ring any bells for you?"

"It sounds like King Arthur," Tom said, thinking Brenna had gone mad.

"That's exactly who it is." Woodsmoke sat up again, staring at Tom intently. "He's been asleep for centuries, and now it seems you must wake him."

Tom stared back at Woodsmoke. "But he died. At least fifteen hundred years ago—if he ever existed at all. And what the hell's he doing here?"

"Oh, he was real, Tom. It is said he will reappear when he's most needed. Our stories say he will awaken here. This is where he was laid to rest, in a tomb on the ancient Isle of Avalon."

Tom felt as if his head was filled with wool, and he repeated, "But he's dead."

"No, he's asleep—a deep, enchanted sleep. In exchange for the sword, Excalibur, Merlin made a deal with the fey, and therefore so did King Arthur, and close to death he was brought here to rest until he was needed again. The island bridges our worlds, or used to. It can only be reached by summoning the Lady of the Lake, who will take you across on a boat. It's old magic, Tom."

"How do you know all this?"

"Because my grandfather is a bard, a teller of stories, and that was his favourite. Arthur was the King my grandfather tried to wake, and it was the reason he was banished."

Tom felt increasingly out of his depth. "The woman told me that, but she said it was the wrong time and he was the wrong person. So why did he try to wake him?"

"He was trying to help a friend. And it seemed like fun."

Tom looked at him suspiciously. "Really?"

"You'll see when you meet him." He rolled his eyes. "But I don't understand why we need the King now."

"She said something about Queen Gavina 'hunting her own.' What does that mean?"

Woodsmoke looked with alarm at Brenna, who went pale and stuttered, "I suppose that means she's killing her own people. But why would she do that?" She stared at Tom. "How are you to wake him? She must have said."

"She told me to use this." Tom produced the silver twig with a flourish. "And she said you would show me the way, Woodsmoke. And that we should hurry."

Woodsmoke took the silver twig off him, examining it closely, before passing it back. "Did she now? I have no idea what this is, but Fahey might. We need to get back home as soon as possible. Come on, let's go." He stood up and gestured down through the forest and to the west. "We know where we are, and that's where we need to go."

Tom stood, put the silver twig in his pack, and extended a hand to Beansprout, pulling her to her feet. She frowned. "I don't understand. Why do you have to do this?"

Tom laughed. "Something about me being his blood."

"What?" she exclaimed. "So you're related to King Arthur?"

"Mmm, I suppose so."

"So I am, too?"

"I don't know. She didn't say."

With a shrug, he strolled off after the others, leaving Beansprout open-mouthed behind him.

The pines thinned out, and became mixed with oak, birch, and beech trees. Spring flowers grew underfoot, and the scent of blossoms filled the air. The powerful feeling of magic had gone, but Tom could still feel a tingle, like static in the air. Woodsmoke strode next to them, setting a quick pace, but Brenna flew. He explained that when they left the wood, they would enter the orchard terraces that ran above the river, adding that he'd heard rumours about attacks from the wood sprites that had left Aeriken Forest to hunt further afield.

Tom laughed. "What? Tiny little wood sprites with bells on their hats? How can they be dangerous?"

"Because they are not small. They have vicious sharp teeth. In fact, they are deadly hunters."

"Oh," was all Tom could think of to reply.

Beansprout smirked. "Idiot."

They walked for hours, and by the end of the day, Tom was exhausted. They'd had no sleep the previous night, and it was only adrenalin that was keeping him going. In fact, they were all tired, and their pace was slowing when they finally reached the broad sprawling terraces, filled with unruly trees covered in blossom. Between the trees the grass grew tall, and they stumbled over fallen branches and abandoned tools.

"What happened here?" Beansprout asked.

"The wood sprites have been busy," said Woodsmoke. "Everyone's abandoned this place. Be careful—we don't know if the sprites are still close."

They progressed steadily, until about halfway down they heard the river roaring in the distance, and saw a collection of stone buildings that looked abandoned.

Woodsmoke looked pleased. "Perfect. We can stay here for the night."

Brenna landed next to them, turning back into human form, and they cautiously entered the closest hut. Inside, baskets were strewn across the floor, and wooden tables had been overturned, suggesting a fight. In the corner was a ladder leading to the upper floor. Brenna pulled her sword free and climbed up, peering slowly over the edge. "It's empty," she called down.

Woodsmoke gestured to Tom. "Come with me, we'll check the other buildings."

Tom was glad to help. He'd felt useless in the cavern

when the dectopus attacked, and now that he'd been told he had to wake the King, he felt he should prove his worth. They searched the place thoroughly, and once satisfied there was no one else there, they strolled to the far edge of the terraces. Woodsmoke pulled out his longbow, saying, "I'll see if I can get us some dinner."

Tom watched him for a few moments and then asked, "Is waking the King dangerous?"

Woodsmoke kept his gaze ahead. "I have no idea, Tom. I'm sure it won't be easy. Did you say you have been having dreams about the Lady of the Lake?"

"Yes, for months. Ever since Granddad disappeared. She told me she's been waiting for me, and that I've taken too long."

Woodsmoke sighed. "Sounds like she's been planning this for some time. I suspect sending my grandfather to your world was part of her plan."

Tom nodded as he realised Woodsmoke was probably right. "But you'll help me get there?"

"Of course. We'll take you to the lakeshore, but I don't know what to expect any more than you do. I wonder what the Queen is up to?" He quickly released three arrows, which disappeared in the long grass. "Dinner," he said, strolling over to pick up the limp rabbits.

The next morning, they carried on towards the river, a ribbon of light in the distance. Tom was distracted by thoughts of the silver twig and waking the King. He didn't know how he was going to do it, but he felt excited at the prospect. He'd read so many stories about King Arthur and his knights, and he tried to imagine what he would be like. Beansprout was lagging behind, because she'd stopped often to gaze across the landscape. Exasperated, he shouted, "Beansprout, keep up!"

She ignored him, giving an occasional wave to keep him happy, and eventually he gave up, figuring she'd catch up when they stopped.

The sun burned hot and the day was still, without a breath of wind. Tom was sweaty and uncomfortable by the time they reached the river, which meandered across the base of the terraces, separating them from the broad flower-filled meadows beyond. Out of the meadows rose a large mound that glowed a vigorous green, and Tom couldn't help but stare at it. It looked uncanny rising out of the long grass.

The river was too wide and deep to wade across, so they headed for a bridge they could see nearby. It was a made from huge stone blocks, and as they drew closer, they saw that big chunks of stone had fallen, tumbling into the river below. Woodsmoke went across first, saying, "Tread carefully, and let's keep some distance between us."

Brenna flew ahead while Woodsmoke kept to the edge by the low stone wall, avoiding gaping holes beneath which the water passed lazily, and Tom and Beansprout followed his lead. At the other side they followed the road through the meadows, and Tom paused, his hand shielding his eyes from the glare of the sun, and squinted at the mound to his left, which he could see more clearly now. It was a perfect half-sphere covered with smooth cropped grass, and was oddly unnatural, but Woodsmoke kept walking, and Tom quickly followed him. As they drew level with it, Tom heard a deep rumbling sound, which travelled through his feet and into his chest, and he stopped and looked around with alarm.

A large dark opening appeared in the side of the hill, and a crowd of strange creatures poured out, heading across the meadows towards them. They were tall, their limbs sinewy with muscle, and there was a faint greenish tinge to their skin. Their blood-curdling cries made it all too clear they weren't there to chat.

Woodsmoke yelled, "Wood sprites! Tom, Beansprout, get behind me!" Ahead of them, Brenna swooped down to the earth, turned back into her human form, and pulled her sword from its scabbard.

Turning, Tom saw that Beansprout was still some way behind them. He couldn't tell if she'd seen what was happening, but hoped she would stay where she was, for her own safety.

Woodsmoke raced across the meadows to Brenna's side and Tom followed, determined to help. He had no weapons, but he didn't care. There must be something he could do.

Even from a distance, it was clear Brenna was ruthlessly attacking the sprites, ploughing through the middle of them, her sword flashing in the sunlight. As Woodsmoke ran, he fired a volley of arrows with unnerving accuracy. The sprites stumbled and fell, trampled underfoot by others.

As Tom grew closer, he could see their lips pulled back as they whooped, their sharp teeth gleaming, but it seemed they were only after Brenna. She edged backwards, towards Tom and Woodsmoke, but there were too many sprites to outrun. A large net was thrown over her, knocking her to the ground, and she disappeared from view.

Tom and Woodsmoke were trapped. Some of the sprites had separated from the pack, blocking them from reaching Brenna. While Woodsmoke fought them with his sword, Tom rolled to the ground, trying to scramble through legs and spears, and he finally fought his way clear, staggering to his feet, bloodied and bruised, only to see the main pack dragging Brenna behind them through the dark doorway. He raced towards them and then, hearing thundering footsteps behind him, dived into the long grass. In seconds the last few sprites passed him, and he heard the groan of the doorway starting to close. With one final effort, Tom threw himself into the narrowing entrance before it clanged shut behind him.

# Chapter 7: Beneath the Hill

Tom lay holding his breath for precious seconds, his face against the ground, hoping he had entered undetected. He heard the sprites' raucous cries, and one of them shouted, "Take her to the store rooms by the kitchen. They're close to the rear gate!"

As their shouts faded, Tom sat up, his back pressed against the doorway.

If he had given any thought to what was inside the mound, he would have imagined a warren of corridors made from earth and rock. But it was far from that. Veins of gold and silver illuminated the walls with a dim light, revealing an ornate, richly carved passageway stretching to his left and right. The roof arched high overhead, from which clusters of glowing, jewel-like stones hung like tempting fruit, while the floor beneath him was shiny black marble. Directly ahead was a broad set of stairs climbing steeply upwards into darkness.

The sprites had headed left, so that was the way he must go. He took a few deep breaths to steady himself and started creeping down the passageway, which followed the curve of the hill. Before long, the light became brighter, and he heard voices and laughter. Peering cautiously around a bend, he saw a small group of wood sprites talking, with no way of going around them. He'd have to turn back and find Brenna another way. She should be safe for now; he had a feeling that if they'd wanted to kill her, she'd be dead already. He decided to try to understand the layout of the mound so that when he found her, he'd know how to get out.

He retraced his steps, following the path to the right. Steps ran off the passage to lower levels, but he ignored them, and soon came to an antechamber with three doors leading off it. He cautiously opened one, and saw that the room beyond glowed with the same faint light. There was no one in sight, and he slipped inside.

The room was magnificent. There were shelves full of books, and more were stacked on the floor, on desks, and on chairs. He ran his hands along their covers and wondered what the strange, curled writing meant. On the walls were carved wood panels and richly embroidered tapestries, but the room had no other doorways—it was a dead end.

The second room was equally magnificent. It was like a reception room, with sofas and well-padded chairs. The third door led to another corridor, but this became so winding and twisted, and there were so many turnings off it, that Tom became afraid he would get lost, so he carefully retraced his steps.

Back in the antechamber he followed the original corridor to the entrance, and paused at the bottom of the staircase, debating if it was wise to go any further. But he had no choice. He had to find a way to get to Brenna. Fortunately, there was no sign of the wood sprites, and Tom was so intrigued at what appeared to be a palace under the hill that he forgot to be afraid. He headed up the stairs, and at the top found another antechamber and an ornate double doorway. He passed through it and entered a huge, mirrored ballroom barely lit by the pale silvery light. He pulled a torch out of his backpack and shone the beam around the room, angling it quickly downwards when shattered light sparkled at him from all directions.

Piles of clothing were strewn across the floor. He picked his way through, and then, stooping to take a closer look, nearly dropped his torch in shock. He leapt backwards, his heart pounding.

These weren't just clothes. There were people inside them.

At first, Tom thought they were dead. But as he looked closer, he realised they were sleeping. Hundreds of them— not actual people, he realised, but faeries, with high, arched eyebrows and a slight point to their ears, lying where they must have fallen, in a deep, enchanted sleep.

Dust lay across their clothes and faces, and flew up from the floor as he walked. He tried not to sneeze. This was the creepiest thing he'd ever seen. With every step he took, he thought one of them would awake and grab him, but he kept moving, his heart pounding and his mouth dry. He could see doorways leading off to other rooms, also filled with enchanted faeries. They had fallen asleep upon chairs and tables, their faces landing on plates of food, their drinks abandoned.

His ears were playing tricks on him, too; he thought he heard whispers as soft, violet-scented breezes caressed his face. He repeated to himself, *they're asleep, they're asleep, keep going.*

Tom crossed to doors on the far side of the room and found that they opened onto a long, broad balcony with stairs at either end. The balcony was also filled with sleepers, and it was here that Tom nearly gave himself away.

Below him was a vast hall, dominated by a cavernous

fireplace in which blazed a huge fire, and it was filled with wood sprites—dozens of them. At the edges of the rooms were more sleepers, piled unceremoniously into heaps. Quickly turning off his torch, Tom dropped down next to the sleepers and crawled forward to peer through the carved railings.

They seemed to be celebrating, probably because they'd captured Brenna. They passed around drinks, shouting and singing, while a smaller group clustered together, their heads close. Tom could smell roasting meat, and his stomach rumbled. A couple of sprites emerged from a door to the right of the fireplace, close to the corner, and they rolled in a large cask, which they manoeuvred to the rear wall.

One of the wood sprites stood and banged his fist on a long table that ran the length of the room. When he had the others' attention, he shouted, "At last we have someone to offer the Queen. We will leave at dark to take her subject to her, and then we will be assured of her help!"

At this, they roared with pleasure.

"Are you pleased, Duke Craven?" He looked to a faerie standing in their midst, dressed in black and with an unpleasant smile on his lips.

"I am, although it is unfortunate it has taken so long. To change!" He raised his glass in a toast, and everyone roared again.

Tom needed to find Brenna and get her out of there, fast. The sprite earlier had mentioned keeping her in the store rooms, and he looked at the cask that was now being emptied rapidly. Casks were generally kept in storerooms, which must mean Brenna was somewhere beyond the door in the corner. But to remain unseen he needed the sprites to stay clustered around the Duke in the middle of the room. Fortunately, the stairs to his right were well away from the crowd. He crawled, belly low to the floor, sniffing dust and grime, down the staircase. He paused for a moment at the bottom, making sure the sprites were still occupied, and then wiggled his way between the sleepers until he reached the deeply shadowed far wall. The sprites were a rowdy bunch, and while they continued to drink and cheer, Tom advanced, trying to ignore the deeply unpleasant feeling of limbs squashing beneath him. Every now and again he paused and flopped, feigning sleep, until he was finally close enough to stand and slip through the doorway.

Tom froze on the other side, pressed against the wall. He glanced around, and satisfied there was no one there, ran along the corridor until he came to steps leading downwards. At the foot of the steps he walked softly down the poorly lit passageway. The ornate decoration of the upper corridors was gone, and through half-open doors he saw storerooms housing boxes, bags of flour, jars, and bottles. Eventually, he came to a closed door. Trying the handle, he found it was locked, but fortunately the key was still in the hole.

He pressed his ear to the door, but it was silent within. "Brenna, are you there?" he called softly.

"Yes, yes, it's me! Tom?"

He unlocked the door, pushed it wide open, and found Brenna already waiting, some rough canvas sacks on the floor behind her. She looked rumpled and slightly grubby, not to mention genuinely shocked to see him, but quickly joined him in the corridor, holding her shoulder stiffly. "How did you find me?" Her sword was gone, and she looked vulnerable without it.

"Long story. Are you injured?" He pointed to her shoulder.

"Yes, but it's not serious."

He nodded. "Good. We have to get out of here. They're coming for you." He locked the door behind them so it looked undisturbed.

She laid a hand on his arm. "No, we can't go yet."

"What? Why not?"

"There's another prisoner, right next door. I heard them speak to him."

"Brenna, we haven't got time! Didn't you hear me? They're coming for *you*! They're taking you to some Queen as an offering!"

Brenna went horribly pale, and fear flared behind her eyes, but she still shook her head. "I don't care. We can't leave him. You know we can't."

"He could be a mad man!"

She just frowned at him. "Or he could be just like me!"

He sighed with exasperation. "But we could be caught any second!"

"We are not leaving without him. Here," she said, removing the key from the door, "I think they used the same key."

They headed to the next room, where the door was once again locked, and she slid the key in, turning it easily.

Inside was a sleeping faerie. He was tied to a chair placed against the far wall, his body secured by rope that wrapped around his arms, legs, and torso. He had long, white-blond hair that shone with a pale light, and wore clothes that had been fine once, but which were now dirty and torn. Tom shook him gently.

The faerie's head shot up and he shouted, "Get away! How dare you touch me!" His eyes were a deep, midnight blue.

Tom jumped back, his hands in the air. "I'm here to help!"

The fey took a long look at him, and then at Brenna behind him. "Who are you? What are you doing here?"

"I am *trying* to rescue you."

He shook himself awake, his eyes bright and eager. "Really? At last!" Then he looked down at the rope wrapped about him. "But I can't leave unless we can remove this!"

"Well, we need to go now, so unless we can do this quickly, we'll have to leave you here." Tom thought through his options. "Maybe I can find a knife."

The faerie shook his head. "No, this may look like ordinary rope, but it's not. My restraint is made from smoke. It's a type of magic, and these coils have to be unlocked. But I know where the key is. I have just enough power left to disguise you so you can get it for me." He looked pleadingly at Tom.

Tom examined the coils and realised they did have a smoky quality up close, but he couldn't see where a key would fit. He looked back towards Brenna, and she nodded. "Tom, we have to!"

He grunted, not entirely seeing the 'we' in this. "All right, fine! Where's the key?"

"Around the neck of my treacherous rat of a brother, the Duke of Craven."

Tom nearly choked. "He's your *brother*? I've just seen him in the hall, surrounded by murderous wood sprites! It would be impossible to get close enough."

Panic shot across the faerie's face. "I can disguise you, I promise! Please. If I don't get out of here soon, he'll find out how to use the Starlight Jewel, and then he'll be too powerful for me to stop! And he'll kill me."

Tom felt his heart sinking. He just wanted to get out of there, but felt he didn't really have a choice. He looked at Brenna where she stood in the doorway, watching their exchange. "If I do this, I'm going to have to lock you back in the room."

"I understand."

Tom sighed. "All right. What do I have to do?"

# Chapter 8: Starfall

The fey smiled at Tom, relief pouring from him. "As I said, Craven has my key around his neck. It's small and looks like glass. It fits here." He jerked his head to one of the coils that lay across his chest. "This binding has reduced my magic, but I can cast a spell that will draw some of this smoke to you and allow you to pass unseen into the hall. The enchantment will hopefully last long enough for you to steal the key and bring it back to me. Once I'm free, I promise to get you out of here."

The word *hopefully* rang in Tom's ears, and he looked balefully at the fey. "How long is long enough?"

"Half an hour or so?"

Tom hoped the Duke was still in the hall or he would never find him, and then he'd be captured, too. "Okay. Do it now."

"Come closer so I can reach you."

Tom knelt next to the faerie to get close to his bound hands, and he pressed his index finger to Tom's forehead. He felt a strange sensation pass through him, and he looked down. His body was suddenly shimmering.

"What on Earth?"

"*Go!*" the faerie urged.

Tom ran out the door, and Brenna locked it carefully

behind them.

"Tom, he's right," she said, going back into the room she'd been held in. "You're barely visible. Just stick to the shadows, and you'll be fine. Good luck!"

*Barely visible* wasn't entirely reassuring, but as Brenna handed him the key, he was relieved to find he could still grip things properly.

After locking Brenna in, he ran back up the corridor. It felt twice as long as before. A sprite appeared before him and Tom froze, but it disappeared into a store room, reappearing moments later with an armful of bottles, paying him no mind. As the sprite went back up the stairs, Tom followed, treading softly, his heart hammering in his chest.

He edged into the hall, trying to get his breathing under control. The sprites were still shouting and singing, some aiming their spears at the far wall, where several figures had been drawn. There was a rhythmical *thump* and cheer as the spears found their mark. Tom wasn't sure if drunk sprites were better or worse than sober ones.

Tom saw the Duke sitting on a chair in the deep shadows cast by the balcony above. He was examining a map spread out on the table before him, illuminated only by the light of a single candle.

Tom again hugged the walls, but nobody was looking in his direction. He couldn't even see himself. He crept closer and closer to the Duke until he was standing behind him. It was uncanny—Craven looked like a photographic negative of his brother. His eyes were dark and his hair was black, with a faint, dusty sheen to it, like diamond dust. Although his features were sharper, they were virtually identical.

The Duke's attention was completely on the map. Tom could see the glass key on a chain around his neck, chinking next to other, bigger keys. He flexed his fingers and tried not to breathe heavily. The Duke leaned back in his chair, closed his eyes, rubbed his face wearily, and then dropped his hands to his sides. Tom seized his moment. He edged forward and reached over the Duke's shoulder, his fingers inches away from the key. The Duke's hand shot up as if he'd felt him, and Tom snatched his hand away, rocketing back against the wall. The Duke opened his eyes and patted his shoulder, confused, then sat up and looked round, scanning the space behind him. Tom stood motionless, holding his breath.

Distracted by an approaching sprite, Craven turned away.

"Duke Craven, we need to go soon," said the sprite.

"Yes, all right, just give me a few more minutes. Are the horses ready?"

"I'll send someone down, they can get the girl on their way back." He strode off, shouting to one of the others.

The Duke pulled a large jewel out of his pocket. It was the size of a duck egg, and its centre glowed. He lifted it level with his eyes and gazed into it. Tom leaned forward too, peering into its depths. He thought he saw swirling stars, and mesmerised, moved closer, halting abruptly as the Duke sighed, re-pocketed the jewel, and then leaned back and shut his eyes again.

Tom's stomach churned. He had to get the key now or it would all be over. He reached forward and pulled the key gently between his thumb and forefinger. The key melted off the chain and into his hands; the key recognised him, it seemed.

Without waiting to see if he had disturbed the Duke, Tom ran back across the hall, down the stairs, and along the corridor. He could tell the spell was wearing off, and he reckoned he only had a few minutes of invisibility left. He heard footsteps behind him and froze, but the sprite entered a doorway without noticing Tom, and he ran again, skidding to a halt in front of Brenna's room.

He quickly released Brenna, and then unlocked the fey's door, with Brenna right behind him. "I've got it!"

The fey was straining against his bonds, a look of sheer anger and frustration on his face. "Quickly, put it where I showed you!"

Tom fumbled with the key. "But there's no keyhole!"

"There will be! Do it *now*!"

He placed the key over the spot the faerie had indicated. Magically, a keyhole appeared, and he slotted the key in and turned it. There was a strange hissing sound and the smoke-rope began to thin and disappear.

"Ahh, you have no idea how good that feels!" the faerie said, as he rolled his shoulders and gingerly stood up. He groaned. "Oh, I am so stiff!"

He limped to the door, where he went to turn left. Brenna was already waiting in the corridor, anxiously keeping watch.

"Not that way," Tom said, grabbing his arm. "There are hundreds of them in the hall, and some are coming any minute now to get Brenna. Is there a back way out?"

The faerie looked thoughtful. "All right, follow me."

He set a quick pace, despite his stiff gait, and the further they went, the faster he moved. They continued down passageway after passageway, twisting and turning until Tom was completely disorientated, before they finally entered a large room. A collection of weapons was mounted on the walls, and cloaks of varying sizes and colours were hung on a row of hooks. On the far side was a sturdy wooden door.

Tom could hear shouts in the distance and he ran over, grabbed the handle, and tried to turn it, but it wouldn't budge. Brenna took over, her hands fumbling with panic.

The faerie looked at them with disdain. "This is a faerie palace. It won't open just like that. Now, who are you?"

"Can't this wait?" Tom asked. "I can hear shouting! They know you've escaped! We have to leave now!"

The faerie gave them a tight-lipped, unpleasant smile that didn't reach his eyes. "I'm not going anywhere. This is my palace and I shall have my revenge. No one knows this place better than me. They caught me by surprise last time, but not again."

"But there are *hundreds* of them. We can't help you anymore. Brenna is hurt, and our friends will be worried." He glanced nervously at Brenna. "If they're okay."

The faerie grimaced and lowered his voice. "Don't worry, you have done more than enough. I can manage now. If I so choose, there will be endless staircases that lead nowhere, corridors that shrink to the size of a mouse hole, doorways that lead only to a howling abyss, or mirrors that steal your reflection and swallow you whole. They will regret ever attacking us. And he will regret ever betraying me."

As he finished, Tom saw over his shoulder two wood sprites running towards them, spears raised. Tom opened his mouth to shout a warning, but the faerie was already turning, and with a flick of his hand and a mutter of something unintelligible, the floor beneath the sprites opened to reveal a gaping mouth full of teeth and blood-red gums. The sprites fell in and with a growl, the mouth snapped closed.

Tom's own mouth fell open in shock, but the faerie smiled smugly. He asked, "You didn't happen to see my subjects, did you?"

"Well yes, actually," Tom said, struggling to concentrate. "They're asleep all over the floor, on the steps, in the ballroom, and the hall. At least, I think they're asleep."

The faerie looked pleased. "Good. And your name?"

"Tom, and this is Brenna."

"And your friends?"

"Woodsmoke and Beansprout," Tom said impatiently, wondering why that mattered.

The fey bowed majestically and kissed Brenna's hand. "Madam, Sir. I am truly indebted. Now, how did you manage to get in?"

Brenna answered first. "I was kidnapped by the wood sprites—I was to be given to the Queen of Aeriken."

Tom looked at her, startled. He hadn't mentioned a name, but Brenna knew which Queen it was. *Maybe there was only one.* He added, "Some sort of exchange for her power, from what I overheard."

"Really? She doesn't normally share her power. I wonder what's in it for her? And why you?" he mused, looking at Brenna.

Brenna flushed and answered quickly. "I have no idea. And your name?"

He squared his shoulders and lifted his chin. "I am Prince Finnlugh, Bringer of Starfall and Chaos, Head of the House of Evernight. Now go, quickly. Avoid the edge of Aeriken Forest. If there are any more of them, that's where they'll be waiting."

Prince Finnlugh muttered and waved his hands, just as Woodsmoke had done under the tower, and Tom heard the door's lock release. Brenna was already ahead of him, and she pulled it open. Outside, night had fallen. Tom hadn't realised they had been in the mound for so long.

The Prince added under his breath, "If ever there was a time for the King, perhaps it is now."

Tom and Brenna stopped at the threshold and looked at him.

"What did you say?" asked Tom.

He looked at them warily. "Nothing, ignore me."

Tom persisted. "You mentioned the King."

"I am merely thinking aloud. Forget I ever said anything."

"Well," Tom said, considering his words carefully, "we're travelling to the lake, if you wish to see us again."

The Prince stared at him and then gave a slow smile. "The lake? What an interesting destination. I shall bear that in mind. By the way, don't worry about being followed. I will make certain they never leave."

Tom nodded, and they stepped through the door. It shut behind them with a *crack*, leaving them halfway up the hill. Tom took a deep breath, inhaling the still night air with relief as he looked at the spread of stars that silvered the sky. "Thank God we're out of there. That has to be the freakiest place ever. I hope Woodsmoke doesn't live in one of those things. Are you okay?"

"Yes, apart from my shoulder. It's really sore. I fell on it when they threw that wretched net on me."

"The Prince asked a good question. Why you? They didn't bother with the rest of us. What did they mean when they called you her 'subject?'"

Brenna glanced away, reluctant to meet Tom's eye. "I have no idea. They probably confused me with someone else. It's nothing, Tom. Just an exchange for power." She changed the conversation. "Didn't you take a bit of a risk just then? The whole King thing?"

He shrugged. "It felt right."

The grass on the hill was smooth and velvety, unlike the meadows below, which were luxuriant with waist-high grasses. Once they reached the bottom, there was no sign of the main entrance, and they searched for the spot where they had been attacked, hoping to pick up Woodsmoke and Beansprout's tracks. The stars gave them just enough light to see, and they eventually stumbled into an area of flattened grass—dotted with the dead bodies of wood sprites. There was a moment of panic, as they wondered if Woodsmoke or Beansprout lay among them, but there was no sign of either one.

Tom took out his torch, holding it low over the ground, and eventually found a faint track leading away from the area. It was too risky to shout out, so they called in low voices, "Woodsmoke, Beansprout."

They hadn't gone far when they came across another dead sprite. They called again, and this time relief swept through Tom as Woodsmoke answered, "Tom, Brenna, is that you?" They saw a tall figure emerge, black against the pale silver of the grass, and ran to his side.

Brenna hugged him awkwardly, protecting her shoulder. "Are you okay?"

"I am, but Beansprout is not so good. And neither are you, by the look of it!"

"It's just my shoulder. I'll recover. Fortunately, Tom is fine. What happened to Beansprout?"

"A spear hit her." He led them to a ring of flattened grass. Beansprout was curled on his cloak, sleeping heavily.

"How did it happen?" Brenna dropped to her knees next to Beansprout, her face worried.

"She got caught in the skirmish, and a spear took a

chunk out of her arm. I've bound the wound, but it bled a lot and was very painful for her. I've given her herbs to ease the pain and help her sleep. She should be better by tomorrow, I hope."

Tom sat next to Woodsmoke on a corner of his cloak. Now that his adrenalin was wearing off, he felt shattered.

Woodsmoke looked at him with surprise. "I can't believe you managed to sneak in there, Tom, never mind get out again! I tried to follow, but the door had already closed by the time I got there, and the magic was too strong to penetrate. I thought you must be dead."

Tom related everything that happened, while Brenna curled up next to Beansprout.

"So, the Queen wants her subjects back." Woodsmoke looked across at Brenna, but she didn't answer. Only the glint of starlight in her eyes indicated she was even awake.

"She sounds horrible," Tom said, but Woodsmoke only grunted, and Tom decided to change the subject. The Queen seemed to be someone neither of them wanted to discuss. "You don't live in one of those hills, do you?"

"Oh no, they are used only by the old royal tribes."

"Good, because it was really creepy. And the Prince was...odd."

Woodsmoke laughed. "Odd and powerful. I have heard many stories, especially from my grandfather. You must ask him to tell you some. He'll love it."

Tom was intrigued. "Who *are* the other royal tribes?"

"There are quite a few, but locally there are Prince Finnlugh's, the Duchess of Cloy's tribe, and Prince Ironroot's. Their palaces are over there." He gestured over the river. "We don't really see them anymore. They hole up in their Under-Palaces, dancing and feasting their long lives away." He stopped, lost in thought.

"And how are we getting to your home?"

"We'll head to the river, a tributary of the one we crossed today, and try to find a boat. It passes through our local village—we live in the wood close by. It will be quicker, and certainly easier. And then we shall go to the Isle of Avalon."

# Chapter 9: Vanishing Hall

Dawn was breaking, a pale green wash of colour spreading across the eastern horizon when Tom woke. Although, he hadn't really slept at all. He was cold and stiff, and was torn between going back to sleep—*for days*—and wanting to get moving, just to be warm. And he was very hungry. It had been hours since he'd eaten, and he had only a few biscuits left.

He rummaged in his pack as Brenna stirred, stretching tentatively. Woodsmoke was already awake, and he nudged Beansprout. She blinked slowly, her face ashen in the early morning light, and struggled to sit up.

"My arm is so sore," she said groggily, wincing as she wiggled it. And then she saw Tom and Brenna, and her face lit up. "You're back! Brilliant! What happened?"

Tom barked out a laugh. "We had an encounter with a mad Prince and blood-crazed wood sprites. You wouldn't believe what that place is like inside!" He jerked his head to the green mound behind them.

"Tom was amazing," Brenna told her. "He rescued both me and Prince Finnlugh!"

Beansprout's mouth dropped open. "Wow. You have to tell me everything!"

"Not now, he doesn't," Woodsmoke said, rising to his

feet to survey the landscape. "We have to get moving. We still have a long way to go."

"I'll have to do it on foot," Brenna said. "I can't fly with my damaged shoulder."

Woodsmoke nodded. "We'll walk to the river, see if there's a boat we can get on. I know we're all hungry, but we should press on first."

They gathered their things and walked through the meadows, Tom telling the others about what had happened in the palace. It helped pass the time, and by midday they reached the tributary of the main river they had crossed the day before. It was wide and placid, and they followed the path that ran along its bank. After a short time, a boat appeared, heading downstream.

It pulled level with them and a man called out, "Is that you, Brenna? Haven't seen you for a while."

Brenna waved. "Fews! How are you? I don't suppose you're taking passengers?"

Fews was grey-haired with a wrinkled, brown face like an old apple. When he smiled, his eyes almost disappeared into his wrinkles, and Tom saw he'd lost most of his teeth. "Well, I don't normally, but I can make an exception for you."

His boat was long, like a barge, filled with sacks and barrels, and he steered it as close to the bank as he could. He shouted, "Sorry, you're going to get wet. I'll end up grounded if I come any closer."

They pulled their boots and shoes off, waded across to him, and one by one he pulled them over the side.

"You must know Woodsmoke?" Brenna said, as she kissed his cheek in greeting.

"I reckon I know your face," he answered, looking Woodsmoke up and down. "You're Fahey's grandchild?"

"I am," said Woodsmoke, smiling.

"Who are these two? They don't look like they're from around here."

"They're humans, come to visit their grandfather, Jack," Brenna answered.

"Oh, I see, we're having some cross-cultural relations, are we? Well, welcome to my boat, and don't squash anything!"

Tom and Beansprout said hello as they clambered into the centre of the boat and settled themselves in the gaps between the sacks, while Woodsmoke and Brenna sat up front with Fews.

He steered them back into the centre of the river. "What you done to your shoulder, Brenna?"

"Had a run-in with some wood sprites by the Starfall Under-Palace."

Fews's smile disappeared. "They're getting closer, then. I hope you got rid of a few?"

"Of course. They came off worse."

"Good. There are far too many around for my liking. Don't know what's bringing them out of the forest, really. Usually don't like it out in the open."

Their voices faded as Tom dozed in the warmth of the sun, the sacks comfortable beneath him, but images from the previous day still raced through his mind. He could see the Prince's malevolent smile, and hear him describing what the palace could do. Once again he realised how far he was from home, and how strange this place was. His stomach rumbled, but eventually even hunger couldn't keep him awake, and finally, he slept deeply.

Tom woke up when the boat jolted. A murmur of voices prodded his consciousness, and his eyes flickered open. It was dusk and the birds called loudly, swooping over the water, black shapes against a pale-grey sky.

He sat up and found that they were surrounded by other boats, moored up and down the river around them, nudging each other in the current. The others were mostly deserted, with just the odd light shining from masts and bows. On either side, high banks blocked his view beyond the river, but overhead he could see bridges crisscrossing back and forth.

Brenna and Woodsmoke stood on the riverbank talking to a short, squat man who looked like a toad. He nodded a few times before hopping from view in one bound.

Tom nudged Beansprout. "Wake up, Madam. We're here, wherever that is."

She roused and stretched, stopping short when her injured arm hurt. "I'm so exhausted. I want a proper bed."

"Well, we might get one tonight, and we might just find Granddad, too."

She sat up quickly at that. "Of course, I forgot. He's going to be surprised to see us. Have you any idea where we're going now?"

"Nope, I'm just doing as I'm told."

"Well, that makes a change."

They made their way to the top of the bank where they could see their surroundings more clearly.

On either side of the river was a sprawling village, its lights twinkling in the dusk. There was a jumble of buildings and market stalls, and walkways and bridges linked the streets and spanned the water. Strange-looking people were milling around, and music and singing drifted through the air. Tom smelled food, and his mouth watered.

Woodsmoke called them over to where he stood at the fork of the road and a bridge. "I'm borrowing a horse and cart to take us home from here. We should be there by midnight." He looked tired but pleased, and ran his hand through his long hair. He had unslung his bow, and it rested at his feet while he flexed his shoulders up and down. Brenna stood next to him, deep in thought as she gazed across the village and the surrounding countryside.

"Where are we?" Beansprout asked.

"Vanishing Village. And that," Woodsmoke pointed across the river, "is Vanishing Wood, where we live."

Beansprout's eyes were bright with excitement. "Can we look around?"

He shook his head. "No time, I'm afraid."

"Is there time for food?" Tom asked. "I'm starving." As if to prove a point, his stomach grumbled loudly.

"That's a good idea," Brenna said, turning to Woodsmoke. "We've got a few minutes. I'll wait here while you get something."

"All right," Woodsmoke agreed. "I'm pretty hungry myself."

They strolled to the nearest stalls and gazed at the displays of food. There was a big roast pig turning on a spit, the fat hissing as it dripped onto the fire, plates full of pies and pastries, and dishes of fruit that looked sweet and juicy.

"I want it all," Tom said, drooling.

"I'll get us some pies," Woodsmoke said, pulling some money out of his pocket. "Trust me, they're good!"

He pointed out a selection to the stall owner, who bagged them up and passed them over. Woodsmoke handed some out and led them back to Brenna. Tom couldn't wait, and he tucked in, groaning with pleasure. He was just starting on his second pie, and beginning to feel more alert than he had in hours, when a horse and cart pulled up next to them, driven by the short, toad-like man. He hopped down and threw the reins at Woodsmoke, saying in a gruff voice, "See you sometime tomorrow then, Woodsmoke. Safe journey."

He took little interest in the rest of them and headed off over the bridge, the strange lollop in his walk making the curve of his upper spine more noticeable.

Woodsmoke jumped up onto the front of the cart and grabbed the reins, while the others climbed into the back, snuggling under blankets.

They trundled along the road next to the river for a short while before Woodsmoke turned onto a bridge, and they crossed to the other side. Brenna slept, but Tom and Beansprout were wide-awake, staring at everything around them. Small lanes tunnelled between the buildings, burrowing into the heart of the village. They were full of strange beings hurrying about their business. The people—*or rather, faeries*, Tom corrected himself—looked like something out of a storybook. Some were tall and stately, and glided along without appearing to walk. Many of them, men and women alike, had long hair, which the women wore elaborately braided and piled on top of their heads. But then there were those who were distinctly *other*. Little people that looked like pixies, olive-skinned and sharp featured, as well as creatures that were half-animal, half-human. A man with the enormous ears of a hare walked past, and Tom thought he saw a satyr down by the river.

Eventually they reached the village outskirts and entered into woodland, where the midges rose in clouds, and before long all they could hear was the jingling of the reins and the clomping of hooves. Darkness had fallen, and the starlight was blocked by the canopy of leaves, but Woodsmoke knew the way well, and he led them confidently along various turns in the road. Occasionally, Tom saw flickering lights in the distance, but they quickly disappeared before he could work out what they were. Then, at last, a mass of golden lights appeared through the trees.

They entered a clearing containing a well, and a grassy area on which several horses were grazing. Lanterns hung from the trees, illuminating a rambling building of wood and stone that spread in a semi-circle around them. Assorted towers sprouted out of it, some short and squat, others tall and spindly, piercing the canopy high overhead. Vast tree trunks lay at various angles to form part of the buildings, and rooms seemed suspended in the branches. It was the oddest collection of buildings Tom had ever seen, and they looked as if they could all topple down at any minute.

Woodsmoke directed the horse through an archway into a well-lit courtyard, pulled to a stop, and jumped down. Tom scrambled after him, leaving Brenna and Beansprout to follow. A door at the base of one of the corkscrew towers flew open, and a figure strode out, saying, "Who's there? We're not expecting guests."

"We're not guests! It's me, Woodsmoke, with Brenna and a couple of friends."

"Oh, by the Gods—you're back! We were wondering what was taking you so long."

The figure strode into view, and Tom saw an older faerie with feathered eyebrows and a shock of white hair shot through with red. He trailed sparks in his wake, and thick black smoke billowed out of the doorway behind him. His clothes were patched and ripped, and speckled with burns and singed edges, and his cheek was smeared with a grey, glittery substance. Tom noticed a wild distraction in his eyes; he looked as if he wasn't quite all there.

"Are you burning the place down, Father?" Woodsmoke asked, with a note of barely concealed impatience.

"No, just experimenting. Have a little faith," he answered. "My, my, my, so you've brought Jack's grandchildren here? How very pleased I am to meet you." He shook their hands and kissed Brenna on both cheeks. His hand was firm and dry, and he smelt of gunpowder. "Well, I'm glad you're back. Your grandfather is somewhere in the main house," he said to Woodsmoke, striding back towards the tower. "I'll leave you to it!"

"Typical," muttered Woodsmoke. "He's more interested in his experiments than in what's happening anywhere else. You go on ahead. I'll sort the horse, and see you in a minute."

They followed Brenna into the house and across a high-ceilinged kitchen lit only by a smouldering fire. They wound their way through room after room and up several stairways inside tree trunks, before coming out into a big, square room dimly lit by candles.

Tom saw two figures in front of the fire. One was standing as if performing to an audience, while the other, Tom's granddad, sat watching and listening. They were both so absorbed that the three of them lingered at the door, hesitating to interrupt. Tom watched his granddad, hardly believing that he was really there. He hadn't changed. He was still grey-haired and ruddy-cheeked, with the slightest stretch of his shirt over a small paunch. But if anything, he looked slightly younger and more vigorous.

The man he was watching was a spritely older fey wearing a soft white shirt with billowing sleeves and tailored black trousers. He had a noble face, and his silver hair, combed and shining, was tied back in a ponytail secured by a black ribbon. He threw his arm wide as he said, "And he flung his club so far and so high that he knocked a star from the sky. It skittered across the horizon, leaving a blazing trail of light behind it until, gathering speed, it fell to earth."

Finally, they were spotted, and Tom's granddad jumped to his feet and shouted, "Tom! Beansprout! What are you doing here?" He was already trotting across the room, arms outstretched and a big grin on his face. "I thought I'd never see you again!"

Tom and Beansprout ran across the room to meet him, and he crushed them each in bear hugs. Tom felt himself become shaky, and had an urge to sit down.

"Hello, Fahey," Brenna said, greeting the other man with a half-hug, betraying the injury to her shoulder.

Tom's grandfather turned to Fahey, his eyes bright and his voice slightly breathless. "My grandchildren, they're here!"

Fahey smiled broadly. "I can see that, Jack. I'm not blind! What are we all standing for? Come on, sit down and tell us why you're here. Longfoot!" he yelled. "Bring us drinks and snacks."

After a bustle of moving chairs, they sat around the fire and looked at each other, a silence falling momentarily as they all wondered where to start. Jack spoke first. "So why—and how—are you here?"

"Perhaps we shouldn't start there." Beansprout winced slightly. "It's sort of an accident. But how are *you*? And how did *you* get here?" He looked so well that she added, "You look great!"

"I am, I am! But you've grown since I last saw you, and it's only been a few months."

"Longer than that, Granddad," she informed him. "It's been over a year!"

Jack looked open-mouthed at Fahey who shrugged and said, "I told you so."

Tom hadn't wanted to criticise, but seeing his grandfather all warm and happy in front of the fire made him suddenly cross. "We've been really worried about you! How could you just leave us?"

Jack looked stricken. "I'm sorry, Tom. I realise it seems thoughtless, but at the time, it felt like the right thing to do."

"But how? Why? Didn't you think we'd be worried?"

"That's why I left the note." Panic crossed his face. "You did see the note, didn't you?"

"Yes, we did, but it was still odd!"

Beansprout interrupted him with a glare. "Tom, maybe we should talk about this later?" She turned to Jack and smiled. "It's so good to see you! I swear you look younger!"

Tom was still fuming, but he bit his tongue. He realised Beansprout was right—now was not the time to argue.

"It's the air in this place, it does marvellous things to you. I've learned to ride a horse!"

"Have you? That's so exciting! And you live here?" asked Beansprout.

"He certainly does," said Fahey. "He helps me with my storytelling."

Tom looked at Fahey with dislike. It was *his* fault his granddad had left them. He was about to say something to him when he saw Beansprout glaring again, so he continued to sit in silence.

Beansprout turned to Fahey and asked, "So, is that what you do, tell stories?"

"I do. I am a bard, and a very good one," he said

proudly.

"Oh, he is—and what stories!" Jack declared, edging forward in his seat. "Tom, you'd love them." He smiled nervously, as if fearing another outburst.

Tom looked at him in stony silence.

While the others talked, Tom fumed. This wasn't the reunion he'd hoped for. He'd expected his grandfather to be worn out and tired, desperate to return home, but he didn't look desperate at all.

Longfoot arrived, a plump faerie in a long frock coat, with a face that was a little mouse-like. His nose twitched ever so slightly, and he had long, quivering whiskers arching over a small pink mouth. He carried a large tray, crowded with glasses of wine and pots of tea, along with a pile of toast and butter, which they all tucked into with relish—even Tom, who although grumpy, was still starving.

When Woodsmoke arrived, he pulled up a chair and sat next to them, and they told Jack and Fahey about their journey. It was a chaotic, much-interrupted story, but before they could tell them about the Lady of the Lake, Woodsmoke stopped them. "Enough. It's late. Everyone's tired, and two of us are injured, so we should go to bed. We can continue this tomorrow." He said this with such finality and authority that no one argued.

Longfoot was summoned, and Tom and Beansprout were escorted to bedrooms, somewhere in the cavernous house.

# Chapter 10: Old Tales

The odd house was old and ramshackle, with warmth that seemed to ooze out of the walls. It creaked and moaned unexpectedly, and seemed to mutter to itself, which gave Tom a restless night full of vivid dreams that chased themselves around and around in his head.

When he woke, he was still grumpy. He brooded and scowled as Longfoot escorted them through the maze of corridors to the first-floor breakfast room, perched in the leafy branches of a large oak tree.

"Stop it, Tom," hissed Beansprout. "You're behaving like a child."

"I am not!" He picked up a plate, and started loading it with a large breakfast from the selection laid out on the sideboard.

"Yes, you are. We haven't seen Granddad for months, and here you are sulking!"

"We've missed him, and he hasn't missed us at all!"

"Don't be ridiculous! Of course he's missed us!" Beansprout shot back.

"Well, it hardly looks like it. Look where he's living!"

"This is a good thing! He's safe and warm, and doing well. What kind of people would we be if we wanted him to be miserable?"

Tom sat down and started to eat, saying nothing.

"Seriously, Tom," she said, sitting opposite him. "What did you think would happen?"

"I don't know," he grudgingly admitted, between bites of delicious honeyed bacon. "I was too busy wanting to find him."

"And now we have," she said, her voice softening. "And he has a whole new life. Isn't that exciting? I think I'm a bit jealous."

He finally met her gaze. "It *is* pretty cool."

"And *you* did this! You knew that someone was in the woods, and you didn't give up. And look where we are!"

He laughed. "Actually, you did this when you stuck your hand in the portal."

She looked sheepish. "Joint effort, then. But, I don't think he'll be coming back with us. You know that, right?"

"The Lady of the Lake warned me of that. I thought she was mad at the time, but obviously not."

Beansprout looked him right in the eye and it seemed as if she was about to say something significant, and then she just smiled. "Well, I'm glad you're not so grumpy anymore."

"I wasn't grumpy!"

"Liar."

Tom poked his tongue out at her and speared some more bacon, and it wasn't long before Fahey and Jack arrived. Beansprout gave her grandfather a kiss on the cheek, but Tom gave him a chastened, "Good morning."

Jack winked. "Morning, Tom!"

For a while they exchanged pleasantries, Jack asking lots of questions about his family, and Beansprout, ever chirpy, caught him up on their news. Tom watched his granddad, and felt his grumpiness recede even further. He really did look well and happy.

Beansprout turned to Fahey. "I love this house! Why is it so unusual, and why do you live in the middle of a wood?"

Fahey took his last bite of scrambled egg and buttery toast, sighed contentedly, and said, "There's quite a story to that. Can I tell you The Tale of Vanishing Hall?"

Tom may have forgiven his granddad, but he wasn't sure about Fahey yet, the architect of this whole thing, and his lips tightened, but Beansprout smiled. "Yes, please!"

Fahey smiled back and began his story. "Once upon a time, there lived a Count—Count Slipple—one of the fey who lived in the Under-Palace of the House of Evernight. The palace was a warren of vast halls, twisted corridors, and shadowy rooms, hidden under the earth in a great, grassy mound. Time moved differently in this place, slipping by quickly like ghosts through walls, and all of its inhabitants were as old as the earth that buried them, although by a quirk of their race, their skin looked as smooth and fresh as thick cream.

"One day, Count Slipple had a terrible argument with Prince Vastness, the head of the House of Evernight. Prince Vastness was powerful and vengeful, and his words carried great power, but Count Slipple was stronger than the Prince realised. Years of resentment rose between them, and their words spat back and forth like fireworks. The air steamed and hissed, and fiery barbs and stings snatched at their skin and scorched their hair, until their clothes hung from them in tatters. Grand faerie noblemen, ladies, and courtiers ran shrieking into dark hollows and hidden corners as the air crackled with harmful intent. Eventually, the evil in their words manifested into a great black tornado from which Count Slipple ran for his life.

"He fled to the stables deep below the Under-Palace and, flinging himself upon his horse, he whispered the magic words. The hillside rumbled and opened above him, starlight pouring through. He raced across the plains and into the tangled woods, pursued by black stallions carrying Prince Vastness and his royal guard. Branches whipped his face and grabbed at his clothes until, in the middle of the woods, he fell from his horse. Exhausted and injured, he lay facedown in the oil-dark earth, the slime of autumn leaves crushed beneath him, the scent of decay heavy in his nostrils. The ground thundered with the hooves of the pursuing horses, and he realised that if they found him, he would die.

"Inches from his eyes he saw an acorn resting on the forest floor, and he imagined how warm and safe he would feel in such a small, tidy space. As the wild screams of the stallions grew closer he reached for the acorn, and holding it in his hand, whispered, 'I wish, I wish, I wish.'

"The next thing he knew, he was cushioned in a cocoon of velvety blackness. He could still feel the thudding of the black stallions and the ground shook beneath him, but he was warm and content. The thundering hooves fell silent, replaced by the taunts and threats of the riders, which carried menacingly across the still glade. He lay there for what seemed like hours, maybe even days, exhausted and weak, sometimes sleeping, other times thinking and regretting.

"Eventually, when he felt better, and when the percussion of hooves and voices had ceased, replaced by the murmur of wind and rain and the creep of roots beneath him, he decided it was time to leave his cocoon. He thought he would wish himself out of it as he had wished himself in, but however hard he tried, nothing happened. Frustrated, he shouted and cursed and uttered magical incantations, but his howls were swallowed by his prison.

"He tried another way, pushing against his boundaries with his fingers, toes, hands, feet, elbows, knees, shoulders and head. As he pushed, he grew and grew, and the acorn grew with him. It was exhausting work, but slowly a crack appeared in the shell of the acorn, and a gleam of gold in the velvety blackness dazzled the Count's bewildered gaze.

"Eventually, there came a time when he stopped growing, but the acorn didn't. It grew around him until it was the size of a room, and the crack in the acorn was the length of his arm. This time, a spear of silver pierced the gloom, cutting the floor in two.

"The Count rested and gathered his strength, admiring the rippled walls that looked like the surface of water. He thought that, as he had no place to live, it would make a fine house, and would hide him from those seeking to find him. But he was also hungry and needed food, so he made the crack wider and wider until he could step out, and found himself where he had fallen earlier.

"He stood under the glow of the moon. Seeing soft green foliage all around, he realised he had lain in the acorn for months. He heard an insistent *splash* and, walking a short distance, saw a spring bubbling up from the ground, and beyond it, deer were grazing. His horse had long since disappeared.

"Smiling, he looked back at the now giant acorn and saw that it was continuing to grow, the roots pushing beneath the ground with blind urgency. Its roof was arched and branches grew from its rounded sides, contorting and twisting into towers that shot vertically upwards, reaching to the stars. The walls were as shiny as a polished apple, and slivers of light slid across its curved walls like a smile.

"The Count slipped through the shadows of the tangled trees, his footfalls soft on the ground. He looked for signs that the Prince or his men might still be watching, wary too of traps in the undergrowth. But apart from the occasional hoots of owls, all was silent. He walked to the edge of the wood, and gazing across the plains saw the grassy mound in the distance. He sighed, knowing he could never return there.

"As the ground mist rose, he walked back across the forest, and the trees announced themselves in the pale dawn light. Beeches and oaks locked branches against intruders, but recognising him as their own, let him pass with an unravelling whisper before knotting themselves again thickly in his wake. Bird calls rose in a mass, and soon he walked through an ever-increasing crescendo of noise back to the acorn that had sheltered him.

"Count Slipple turned his back on the Under-Palace that night and became Lord Vanishing, and the acorn became Vanishing Hall. In time he took a wife and had many children, grandchildren, and great-grandchildren, and it wasn't until he was on his deathbed that he told them who he really was, and what lay beneath the great green mound in the distance.

"And all of his descendants lived to an uncanny old age. Their skin had a creamy whiteness, their eyes a vivid green that captured the fruitfulness of the forest, and their tempers were as vicious as the summer storms that lit the landscape with the flash and sizzle of lightning."

By the time Fahey had finished his tale, Tom was convinced he could see the whole scene playing out in front of his eyes, and he shook his head, dazzled.

"So this house is from that acorn?" Beansprout asked, also looking as if she'd emerged from a vivid dream. "That's so amazing! And does that mean you're a descendent of Lord Vanishing?"

"Yes, I am. Our whole family is, in fact! But our line has been much diluted since then." He beamed at Beansprout. "But, what a beginning!"

Even Tom had to admit that was interesting.

Woodsmoke, who had walked in unnoticed, so engrossed were they in the story, said, "Are you telling tall tales again, Grandfather?"

Fahey looked slightly put out. "It's not a tall tale, and I shall show you the original room later." He turned to Beansprout and Tom. "It's slightly damp now so we don't use it much anymore. Obviously it's been built on over the years, bits added by different generations, but it's essentially the same place, and every now and then a new tower will sprout or an old one will collapse. It's a wonderful place to live. In fact, when I was away, the old spindle tower completely disappeared." He sighed and a shadow briefly fell across his face. "I missed this place."

Jack patted his shoulder. "Don't think of that time, Fahey. You're back now."

Woodsmoke looked rested. His long, dark hair was clean, and he wore a fresh shirt and dark trousers tucked into his polished leather boots. He joined them at the table with a plate of bacon and eggs and a huge mug of tea. "Speaking of old tales, we have something to tell you. Tom met the Lady of the Lake, and she gave him a job to do."

Fahey slapped the table and looked at Woodsmoke with ill-concealed hunger, and a touch of wariness. "Did she! What did she want?"

"He has to wake the King."

Fahey turned slowly to look at Tom, his eyebrows rising

above his quizzical gaze. "Well, now! That *is* interesting! And what did you say?"

Tom shrugged. "I didn't have much choice. She didn't really wait for an answer."

He told them what had happened in the Greenwood, but had barely finished when Jack interrupted, his fist pounding the table. "No! You will not do it! I won't have you put in danger." He rounded on Woodsmoke. "He shouldn't even be here! This is your fault."

"It is not Woodsmoke's fault at all!" Tom shot back, shocked at his granddad's response. "It's *yours*! She's been visiting me in my dreams for months, ever since you left. You started this!"

His granddad looked surprised. "Well, I didn't ask her to! And how can she visit your dreams? That's ridiculous!"

Fahey intervened. "She's a powerful woman; she can do lots of unexpected things. She put me in a tree!"

Woodsmoke refused to rise to Jack's accusation, and instead spoke calmly. "It seems to me that she sent you, Fahey, someplace where she knew she would eventually find you, Tom. Or at least one of your bloodline." He frowned as he thought through the possibilities. "I think that you, Jack, were unfortunately caught up in it, and that is why she's become so annoyed at how long this has taken."

"Well, she should have been a bit more direct, then," Tom said, annoyed.

Woodsmoke shrugged. "It's probably quite tricky to communicate with more clarity and speed when she has to cross worlds to do so. Tell them what happened."

Tom described his encounter in the Greenwood and what the wood sprites were threatening to do with Brenna in the House of Evernight. He ended by saying, "So, I have to do this, really, whether I like it or not. And besides, Prince Finnlugh, Bringer of Starfall and Chaos, might be able to help."

"Well, well, well." There was a fire burning in Fahey's eyes now. "You think the Prince might help? Maybe he will, but you can't always rely on the old Royal Houses, Tom. They have their own interests. Show me the silver twig."

Tom had put it in the large front pocket of his sweatshirt, so he pulled it out, and slid it across the table.

Fahey moved to the window to examine it in the shafts of sunlight, and then looked at Tom, grinning. "The Silver Bough. It seems you are very special."

"I am?"

"This is a powerful charm that will give you some protection as you travel through this realm. But Tom, don't underestimate how hard this will be, even with this to help."

Tom nodded, remembering The Lady of the Lake's words. "She said it would help me wake King Arthur. I can't imagine how."

Jack sighed. "I still don't want you doing this. This isn't your fight."

"Actually," Woodsmoke said, "it is now. You don't refuse the Lady of the Lake. And besides, Tom hasn't told you the most interesting part yet. Apparently he's related."

Fahey frowned. "To whom?"

"The King."

Jack spluttered. "How can you possibly be related to King Arthur?"

"I don't know!" Tom protested.

Fahey returned to his chair, and Jack warily picked the Silver Bough up, as if it might bite. Fahey's smile, however, held the gleam of intrigue. "This is very exciting. You are a descendant of King Arthur and have been chosen to wake him. This smacks of old magic. Powerful magic! It will be my pleasure to help."

"It will?" Tom asked, surprised. Fahey's response was not what he expected. And apparently, Jack was surprised, too.

"You will? But, but—it's dangerous!"

"All the best stories are."

Jack looked across at Beansprout. "I suppose you'll go, too? Even though I don't want you to."

"Sorry, Granddad, but yes." She looked sheepish as she added, "You came here without asking anyone!"

Tom glared at him. "Yes, you did."

Jack pushed away from the table and paced around the room, running his hands through his hair just as Tom did when he was thinking. He muttered to himself, "Well, it's a fine example I gave, I suppose."

"You did say you wanted adventure, Jack," Fahey pointed out.

"I know I did. But you were spelled into a tree when you tried this!"

"Because it wasn't my time," Fahey said gently. "It's Tom's."

Everyone turned to look at him, and Tom felt horribly self-conscious. And nervous.

"Well, in that case, I'm going, too," Jack announced.

Woodsmoke groaned. "I would try to talk you both out of it, but I know it's pointless. We need to make some plans. We'll take the horses, and enough supplies to keep us going for a couple of weeks. We have plenty of stores and dried meats to choose from."

"But I can't ride a horse!" Tom said. "And neither can

Beansprout."

"That's okay. You can ride behind Brenna and I. And we can teach you on the way." Woodsmoke frowned as he continued to plan. "We'll need to take a few more weapons too, and I can give you some lessons in sword-fighting. Maybe we should start with a few basic defence lessons before we leave. And you both need more clothes, and boots."

Beansprout perked up. "Can we go back to the village to get them?"

"We'll have to. You need cloaks, too."

"We have no money," Tom pointed out.

"I do," Jack said. "I'll pay. I can give you a tour. There's a particularly nice pub we can try, with a very good selection of beers!"

Fahey nodded, looking excited. "You're right there, Jack! I should come, too."

"I should have known a pub would come into it," Woodsmoke said, laughing. "We'll leave in a few days to give Brenna time for her shoulder to recover, and your wound too, Beansprout."

*Sword-fighting!* Tom sat watching vacantly as they talked. He couldn't believe his ears. This was actually happening. He was going to wake King Arthur. He needed air, and space to think. He pushed his chair back from the table, and said, "I'm just going to take a walk."

Tom found his way to the ground floor, and exited through the kitchen and into the courtyard they had entered the night before.

It was a beautiful day; cool in the shade, but hot in the sun. The sky was blue and the trees were flush with bright green leaves. It was difficult to believe they were somewhere other than the land he was so familiar with, and yet as he looked at the Silver Bough in his hands, he felt the world tilt slightly.

This was not familiar. He was in a strange place, being asked to do things he didn't quite understand. It was supposed to be simple—find Granddad and go home. But now he had a job to do, a potentially dangerous one.

He headed past the stables, hearing the snickering of the horses, and then beyond the twisted tower where Woodsmoke's father lived, ending up in the woodland. He meandered until he eventually found a large, flat rock in a patch of sun, behind which was a tangled thicket of trees. This must be the boundary of Woodsmoke's land. He lay on the rock, basking in the heat, and mulling over his future.

*How long had the Lady of the Lake been planning this?* All those dreams he'd been having for months. But then he remembered what Fahey had said the night before. Time passed differently here.

His thoughts were interrupted by a voice calling some way behind him. It was Beansprout, sounding worried.

"Tom, where are you? It's me."

"I'm here," he yelled, not moving.

He heard a rustle and felt a thump, and opened his eyes to see Beansprout wriggling onto to the rock next to him. "I was worried. How are you?"

Tom put his hands behind his head and squinted at her. "I'm contemplating my future. What could be my short future."

"It will be fine," she told him, but her tone didn't carry the conviction of her words. "Surely if she wants the King woken, it can't be that hard. She doesn't want you to fail."

"You'd think not, but everyone seems to think it will be dangerous, and if I'm honest, the Lady of the Lake sounds a bit slippery to me."

Beansprout regarded him solemnly. "True. I'd do it, use your twig thingy, but she didn't ask me."

Tom pulled the little silver twig out of his pocket and turned it slowly in his hands. "It's weird, isn't it? I feel a bit manipulated, really."

"I think we all have been. But Tom, you're descended from King Arthur! Has that sunk in? It's amazing. He exists, and you're going to wake him up. And look where we are." She threw her hands wide, an expression of wonder on her face.

Tom sat up. "I know you're right. But what if she's wrong, and I'm not meant to do this? Or worse, what if I am and I fail?"

"Stop doubting yourself. You can do this, and we'll all help."

"Thanks," he said, smiling weakly. "But then what? I have to wake King Arthur because she needs his help with some crazed Queen who's murdering her subjects. Will we need to be involved with that? That really does sound dangerous."

"Well, I guess we'll soon found out. And I know you're unsure about this, but I'm really glad we're here. Anyway, I'm going to leave you in peace, unless you want to walk back with me?"

"Not just yet, but I won't be long."

She nodded and slipped off the rock. "Later, then."

He watched her go, and then lay back down on the rock, feeling its warmth beneath him and the sun on his face, as he held the bough loosely in his hands. He could hear the wind in the treetops; it sounded like voices, a soft muttering of encouragement for the leaves to grow. He could hear the movement of small creatures in the earth below him, and something like a pulse, similar to hearing his own blood moving through his body. He could feel the bough, warm beneath his fingers.

A sudden image shot into his mind, of an island: fields of fruit trees, golden wheat, flowers and bees, and in the centre a large, dark, deep cave. He felt dread in the pit of his stomach, like a nightmare, and opened his eyes again quickly to chase away the image. He desperately hoped it wasn't what he thought it was.

# Chapter 11: The Hidden Isle

The shadows around them lengthened and the air grew cool as the day drew to a close. A chill wind carried the smell of rain and wet earth across the tufts of springy grass and purple and yellow heathers that covered the moor. Huge rocks, blunt and misshapen, rose from the ground, some big enough to offer shelter. Ahead of them was the massive granite formation of Fell Tor.

They had all been travelling for well over a week, steadily climbing to higher ground. Vanishing Wood was far behind them and the summer weather had disappeared. Tom was aching, cold and saddle-sore. No matter how many layers he wore, the wind seemed to find its way through them, and it wasn't until they sheltered at night he could even begin to get warm.

The night brought its own problems. The wind carried howls, whispers, and threats. The fire they huddled around gave off only a meagre amount of light, as if the surrounding darkness was sucking it up. With nightfall, the ground mist rose and ghostly figures appeared, standing just beyond the edge of the firelight, watching and listening. When they emerged, Tom felt the hair on the back of his neck prickle, and goose bumps rise along his skin. Woodsmoke, Brenna, and Fahey took little notice of the watchers, but Tom,

Beansprout, and Jack were nervous and slept badly, even though they maintained a night watch.

One night, Beansprout had asked if the watchers were real.

"Of course they are," Fahey had said, "although they can't touch you—they're not real in the sense that we are. They are—" he'd leaned forward for emphasis, raising his feathered eyebrows, "your guilty thoughts, brought to life by the dark night."

"They're *what?*" she had asked, alarmed and confused.

"Every little lie, harsh word, or unfair judgement. They're out there, watching."

For a moment, they had all looked beyond the light of the fire, wondering what they had done that caused a figure to be standing there, before quickly dropping their eyes to the fire again.

However, now Tom was so tired that he knew he'd sleep well tonight, regardless of who or what the figures were. The party were aiming for the foot of the Tor where Woodsmoke had assured them there was a cave offering proper shelter. From there it was another half a day's ride to the lake.

Tom adjusted his position. A horse had to be the most uncomfortable method of transport. As Woodsmoke had promised, Tom was riding behind Brenna, and Beansprout was behind Woodsmoke. His grandfather and Fahey, however, rode well, looking comfortable on their own mounts. He tried to adjust his movements to the horse's gait, but failed miserably. He gave up and bumped along painfully. By late afternoon they had reached the base of Fell Tor, and Tom dismounted with a groan.

"I don't think I'll ever get used to this."

Brenna laughed, as she started taking their packs off the

horse. "You will. It just takes time."

Woodsmoke helped Beansprout down, and then pulled free a couple of long torches that were strapped to his saddle bags. He sheltered in the entrance of the cave and used his flint to light them with well-practised ease, as Tom watched enviously. He'd been practising, but wasn't as deft as Woodsmoke.

"Here you go." He passed Tom a torch, and together they inspected the interior while the others unpacked their supplies.

The cave was large and dry with plenty of room for them to spread out, and satisfied that there were no hidden exits, Woodsmoke helped Tom build the fire.

"We're taking a walk up the Tor," Jack told Tom as he brought in their saddlebags. "I want to see the lake, and it will be good to stretch my legs."

Tom nodded. "I'll join you soon."

When they were alone, Woodsmoke asked, "How are you feeling, Tom? You've been quiet for the last few days."

Tom blew on the embers, watching with satisfaction as the kindling caught ablaze. "I'm okay, I suppose. Just feeling more nervous the closer we get."

"That's not surprising. You have no idea what's going to happen when you get there. I confess, I'm a bit worried myself."

Tom snorted. "Not as much as me!" He lifted his gaze from the flames and looked into Woodsmoke's steady brown eyes. "What if I fail?"

"Then the King stays asleep and life carries on. But you won't fail."

"You don't know that. You're being kind."

"No, I'm not. I've watched you. You're resourceful,

stubborn, and you want to learn. You can do this."

Tom summoned his courage and said, "It's more than just nerves. I think I'm scared."

"You should be. That's a good thing. If anything, it will keep you safe. Whatever you do, think first, act later." He laughed dryly. "Sometimes, they both happen really quickly. And have a little faith in yourself. You got this far already."

Tom nodded. "Thanks. I suppose I did."

"Have you had any more dreams lately?"

"Not since we left Vanishing Hall."

"She must know we're coming, which means we won't have to wait long when we reach the lakeside."

"And then what?"

"Your adventure really begins!" He smiled. "Go and join the others. I'll start some food."

Tom grimaced. "I'm not sure I want to! It's cold out there."

"But the view will be worth it."

The wind blew fiercely as Tom rounded the rough path that circled the Tor, and he pulled his heavy woollen cloak around him. About halfway up he found the others sheltering in a hollow, and he huddled next to them. They were looking at the silver shine of the lake in the distance, a shine that stopped abruptly as it met a wall of mist.

"I've just been explaining about that mist," Fahey said to him. "It never goes away. No matter how hot the day, it's always impossible to see the island in the centre."

Tom frowned. "Are you sure it has an island?"

"So the old tales say."

"Has anyone tried to land on it?"

"'Course they have, but it's impossible to sail anywhere on that lake. You think you're making headway, and then the shore is suddenly back in front of you again. I tried for hours, only to end up back where I started. Until of course... *Boom!* I suddenly found myself trapped in a tree, in your realm." He didn't look at them, his attention wrapped up in the lake and the past.

"Are you sure it was the Lady of the Lake who did that?" Beansprout asked.

"Of course I am. She's its guardian. King Arthur's guardian. No one goes there without her bidding."

"Why did you even try?" Beansprout asked, confused.

Fahey looked shifty. "I wanted to help a friend. King Arthur has a reputation as a defender of the weak, and a fair man, as well as a strong one. And well, it's said that he will return when he's needed most."

"You paid a high price, though," Brenna said softly.

He patted her arm. "It was worth trying, and I'm back now." And then he winked at Tom. "But Tom's going to wake him, anyway!"

Tom grunted and looked at the moor below them. It was desolate, its wide expanses of wind-flattened greenery relieved only by blunt-headed rocks rising like whales from the earth. At the lake's edge was a circle of standing stones. They must be huge, because even from here they were an impressive sight.

"Have you seen those, Beansprout?" he asked, pointing at them. "They remind me of Stonehenge."

She nodded. "Amazing aren't they? I can't wait to get down there and see them close up."

"What's Stonehenge?" Brenna asked.

"A very ancient stone circle. Everyone is fascinated by it, even now, and it's been there for thousands of years," Beansprout explained. "There are hundreds of stone circles where we come from."

Fahey stirred. "Come on, let's go before we freeze to death. We'll be there soon enough."

They came upon the circle at midday. The stones looked as if they had stood there for centuries, solid and unyielding to the weather and the passage of time. Carvings jostled for space on every stone, reminding Tom of the carvings under Mishap Folly at home. In the centre of the ring was a smooth area made only of white stone.

They set the horses free to graze, and then walked to the lake's edge, forming a straggling line along the narrow beach. As they gazed across the water, Tom asked his friends, "What now?"

Fahey pointed to the wall of mist. "Someone's coming."

The curved bronze peak of a prow emerged first, topped by a roaring dragon figurehead, its fierce eyes glaring across the water, and Tom's heart skipped a beat. The boat glided through the water without a ripple. A huge square sail stretched across the middle of the boat, filled with wind, even though—for a change—there wasn't so much as a breeze blowing, and it eventually stopped a short distance from the shore.

The Lady of the Lake stepped into view, her long, silver hair flowing around her shoulders and across her vivid green dress. She looked regal and imposing, and she raised her arm and pointed at them.

Tom stumbled and fell to his knees, his hands clutching his head, which felt as if a tight band had been wrapped around it. She spoke directly to his mind, saying, *"Tom, you need to come with me.*" The pain was so intense, Tom thought he might throw up.

The others were unnaturally silent and motionless, gazing towards the boat, but Beansprout rushed to his side. "Tom, are you all right?"

"I can hear her, *right in here*. Can't you? Damn! It didn't hurt like this the other day."

"No, I can't hear anything. What's she saying?" Beansprout turned to glare at the Lady of the Lake and yelled, "Stop it! You're hurting him!"

Immediately, the pain receded, and he straightened up. "Thanks. I don't think she meant to hurt me. It's okay now. She wants me to go with her."

"Go *where*?"

"Where do you think? The island on the lake!"

"On your own? What about me? *Ow!*" Beansprout clutched her head, too.

"What did she say?" Tom asked, guessing what had caused the pain.

"She told me to wait."

He smiled nervously at Beansprout, and his nausea returned. "I'm on my own, then." He stood up, uncertain of his future, and hesitant to go anywhere, but he knew he must. He patted his backpack and checked that he still carried the Silver Bough, and then glanced to his friends and Granddad. "I'm not sure what's happened to them, but say goodbye for me. Wish me luck."

Beansprout threw her arms around him, hugging him tightly. "Good luck, and see you soon!"

Tom tugged his boots off and walked across the narrow beach and into the water, every step taking him deeper, until the water lapped his thighs. When he reached the boat, a rope ladder was waiting for him, and he climbed it, hauling himself over the side. As soon as Tom's feet touched the deck, the boat started to move as the sail flapped and turned. He waved forlornly at Beansprout and saw her wave back, and then the shoreline disappeared as he became enveloped by the mist.

Every time Tom breathed in, moisture rushed into his mouth and lungs, until he felt saturated. The mist pressed into his skin, eyes, and hair, and beads of water formed on the hairs on the back of his hands. His jeans were already soaked through, and he shivered in the cold. The ends of the ship were invisible, and he couldn't even see the water below. He couldn't even detect movement. There was no wind, no sign of rippling water, and no noise of any kind that might indicate where land was. For all he knew he was motionless, stranded in the middle of the lake, freezing to death.

He looked for the Lady of the Lake, but she had gone, and he stood alone. It was a very un-boat-like vessel. There were no stores or ropes, no helm or anchor. Seeking shelter, he looked for a hatch in the deck, but saw nothing except wet planks of wood. He decided it was pointless to keep standing. No matter how hard he looked, the mist was impenetrable, so he sat with his back against the mast, his pack in the small of his back, and wrapped his cloak around him, grateful for its warmth. At least his head felt better now that her voice was out of it. He tried to remember her exact words, but struggled, as if he had heard them a long time ago. Now he knew *what* he had to do, just not *how*, but there was nothing else he could do at the moment, so he closed his eyes and tried to rest.

Tom was awoken by the boat scraping across the ground. He had no idea how long he'd been asleep. He was cold and stiff, and it was only with difficulty that he pushed himself up off the deck to see where he was.

The mist had cleared to reveal a pale blue sky, although tendrils still ribboned through the air and wrapped themselves about the rocks on the shore in front of him. Gnarled trees lined the beach, and beyond them were steep hills thickly clad in tangled trees and bushes. To his right, a narrow crevasse punctured the smooth line of the hills.

Tom was utterly alone. The only sound was of an unseen bird calling high above, its cry eerie and forlorn, emphasising his solitude. The waves hushed insistently against the shingle, and Tom realised he was going to have to get wet again. He slid over the side of the boat and waded to the shore, then tried to squeeze the water out of his trousers before pulling his boots back on.

After surveying his surroundings, Tom realised there was only one place he could go, so he headed to the rocky gap between the hills. The shingle slid beneath his feet, making his movements awkward, but once he entered the crevasse, the ground flattened and hardened and he picked up his pace, anxious to get to his destination—wherever that was. After a while, the path climbed and curled around the hill, until he finally emerged into a clearing and saw a broad vale below, filled with fertile fields, green meadows, and trees. It was the scene from the dream he'd had on the flat rock, and although it was beautiful, his stomach tightened with dread. On the far side of the vale he made out a long, low building of golden stone, glowing in the sunlight, while in the centre stood a rocky hill and the dark mouth of a cave. Tom was hot and thirsty, so he drank from a bottle of water he carried, and started on the path into the valley.

The light was already falling, the sun sinking rapidly, when he reached the valley. The Lady of the Lake appeared ahead of him, and she made sure he had seen her before she turned and walked towards the cave.

"Okay, so you want me to follow you? I get it," Tom muttered, picking up his pace.

The woman flitted like a ghost through the silent landscape, always just ahead of him. No matter how he hurried, he couldn't seem to get closer. Arriving at the cave, she stepped in and disappeared.

Tom was only minutes behind her, and he stopped at the threshold and peered into the murky gloom. She was waiting in the shadows beyond a small fire burning in the centre. To the left was a cavernous hole in the ground, and Tom could see the start of a narrow staircase descending into the blackness.

Now that he was actually face to face with her, Tom could see that she was of average height and slim build. Her silver hair flowed over her shoulders, framing her petite, oval face that was neither young nor old. Once again, Tom had the impression of great age, but it was hard to tell physically.

He took a few steps inside. "What is this place?"

For the first time she actually spoke out loud, and her voice was as commanding as it had been in his dreams. "This is Avalon, the Isle that bridges worlds. It is the place where things begin, end, rest, wait, and watch."

"Well, that sounds suitably weird. And I suppose I'm going down that?" He pointed to the hole in the ground.

"Yes, it leads to the tombs of many creatures, from many races."

"Oh, fab," he said dryly, feeling his stomach churn.

"And what happens when I find King Arthur?"

"You will lead him back to the surface. He has to stop the Queen. She is destroying everything. Once you wake him, he must go to the Old Forest."

"Will he even know where that is? I don't!"

"Your friends will know. They can lead him." She was frustratingly calm, as if he were asking ridiculous questions.

"But why *me*?" he persisted, feeling a dreamlike quality steal over him, despite the realness of his surroundings. "Why blood? And how do you know I'm related? You might be making it up!"

She lifted her chin. "I never joke about matters as important as this. You bear the mark, do you not? A dark, sword-shaped birthmark across your arm."

Again, Tom had a feeling of being out of his depth; a pawn in someone else's game. His hand moved subconsciously over his deltoid and the long birthmark. "How do you know that?"

"I put it there. Merlin insisted that whoever woke King Arthur must be related by blood. It was one of his conditions during our negotiations, and so it was woven into the spell."

*Merlin! Spell...* Tom could barely believe what he was hearing.

Before he could speak, images appeared in Tom's mind of an old man and a young woman, sitting around a fire at the edge of the lake, under a star-filled sky. Between them was a long, silver sword, flashing with firelight and shadow.

*The old man shouts, "Vivian! I insist. If he must awake here, he must not be alone. One of his kin must wake him."*

*"You are a sentimental old fool. He will not be alone!"*

*"If you deny this request, I deny you him!"*

*"And I keep the sword."*

*He pleads, "Please, he is like my son."*

*She hesitates, and eventually nods. "Then his descendants will be marked, and I shall follow them all." She reaches into a bag at her side and pulls out herbs and a small cauldron, and together they start to chant.*

Tom shook his head and blinked. "Was that you? You're Vivian?"

"A very young me, yes."

"But you aren't one of them. The fey. What are you?"

She smiled, making her look younger. "I am human, like you. I dedicated my life to magic and the great Goddess, and decided to stay here, a very long time ago. I helped negotiate the sword."

"But why me?" he insisted.

"I followed all of you through the years, not sure when the time would be right. Any circumstance could have eventuated the need for his return, but current events have deemed that *now* is the time. And so I watched … With difficulty, I must add. Some of you were too old, some too young, most too weak. I took a chance with your family, and when Fahey tried to get here, I sent him to your world, to wait until I was ready. I thought he could he show one of you the way."

"You put him in a tree!" Tom said, incredulous.

"I could have done worse," she replied ominously.

"But he didn't bring me, did he? I was left behind, and my granddad came instead."

Her demeanour suddenly changed and she shouted, "Have you any idea how complicated that spell was? What Merlin demanded? It was ridiculous, and I knew it was, but I gave in to him anyway, as I always did! The boundaries between worlds were like gossamer then, but not anymore. I no longer have the power to influence events beyond these borders. And now it has taken too long and you must hurry!" Her voice rose with annoyance.

"Wait! I have more questions!" Tom had no idea if he would ever see this woman again, and he needed to understand. "Do you mean my granddad and my dad are also descendants, and Beansprout, too?"

She nodded. "Yes, all of you."

"Why didn't you use my granddad then? He was already here."

"He's too old. What I ask you to do requires youth and strength. And your father is too set in his ways."

"What about Beansprout?"

"She too has merits, but I see a different future for her. I chose *you*."

Tom felt a sudden rush of dizziness at the implications of her words, and feeling a little sick, he glanced at the dark opening and said, "So, I suppose it's time?"

She smiled. "Have faith, Tom. I chose you for a reason. Follow the steps to the bottom, and then go along the passageway. His is the final tomb, and the first. Remember to use the bough I gave you. It will help you speak to Arthur, too."

He noticed that she dropped his title, a sign of her friendship with him perhaps. "How do I find my way in the dark?" He had visions of his torch battery failing and leaving him alone in the blackness.

She leaned forward and pulled a flaming branch from the fire, muttered a few words over it, and then handed it to Tom wordlessly. He took it and headed towards the steps, wondering why he'd allowed himself to become involved in such madness.

As he started down the steps, she shouted, "Do not turn off the main path!"

*Great,* he groaned to himself, as he descended into darkness. He was going to get lost and die down here. *So much for destiny.*

# Chapter 12: The Lakeside

For a few minutes, Beansprout stood watching as Tom disappeared into the mist, heading to some distant place she would never know.

A chill swept through her. The boat was clearly ancient; it reminded her of images she had seen in history books. Its familiarity scared her—it was as if the past had crossed an invisible barrier and was suddenly right next to her. It challenged everything she had ever known.

Trying to shake off the feeling, and realising there was nothing she could do now to help Tom, she hurried across to where the others stood, still motionless. She stopped in front of her grandfather. His eyes were filled with tears and he gazed beyond her, into the distance. She hesitated, wondering if it would be dangerous to disturb him and the others, but decided she couldn't just leave them standing there.

She reached out her hand and laid it gently on his arm. "Granddad, wake up." He remained motionless, so she shook him, watching his eyes carefully. "Granddad, can you hear me? It's me, Beansprout." She thought she detected a flicker of movement in his eyes, but then it was gone.

She sighed and moved to Woodsmoke. He was much taller than her, so she couldn't see his eyes properly. Feeling self-conscious, she touched his sleeve and then his hand, shaking it. "Woodsmoke, wake up."

He didn't stir and she sighed again. With her back to the wide expanse of grey water, she looked at the desolate moor, the windswept grass, the trees, knotted and bent, and the tall standing stones, mysterious and indifferent to her needs. She felt overwhelmingly lonely.

She panicked. "Woodsmoke, I'm scared. Don't leave me here alone!" She shook him more aggressively, and felt a pressure on her hand as he squeezed back. He shook his head as if emerging from a deep sleep, blinked a few times, and then looked down at her. She suddenly became aware that she was still holding his hand, and released it quickly, asking, "Are you okay?"

"I think so. I had the weirdest dream." He looked around. "What's going on? Where is Tom?"

"Gone. With her. And you've been bewitched. All of you." She nodded at the others. "I couldn't wake Granddad."

"And what are we supposed to do?" He moved in front of Jack, Fahey, and Brenna, looking at their frozen faces.

"We have to wait for Tom. Shall we try and wake them? And then we can set up camp."

Brenna and Jack roused more quickly than Fahey, who seemed to be in the deepest sleep. Slowly, smiles played across his face, and it was with the greatest reluctance that he finally woke up, annoyed to leave a perfectly good dream.

It seemed wrong to set up camp within the standing stones, so they found a spot to the side of them, behind the narrow beach. They rigged up a waterproof shelter and built a fire of dry brushwood collected from along the shore. It was mid-afternoon by the time they had finished, and they sat around the flames together, warming their hands and drinking a strange herbal tea that Beansprout didn't really like, but had managed to get used to.

Beansprout asked Fahey, "What did you see while you were bewitched? It took ages to wake you!"

He shook his head with wonder. "I saw all the old tales I know, right in front of my eyes! They seemed so real that I didn't want to wake. I saw details that I never knew, and that I can now share with others!"

"What about you, Granddad?"

"I floated over the Realm of Earth," he told her, a faraway look in his eyes. "So many amazing places that I haven't seen." He looked at Fahey. "Places we should go when we have the chance."

Fahey nodded. "Why not? Sounds fun. What about you, Woodsmoke?"

"I was hunting in the Old Forest, a place I haven't been for years. It was good to be back there, and it woke many old memories." He turned to Brenna. "And you? You were upset when you woke."

She shuddered. "I dreamt I'd lost my wings. It was horrible. I couldn't fly anymore. That's why I took off as soon as I woke. I needed to feel the air again." She shrugged, as if fluttering her wings, even though they weren't there at that moment. Beansprout wondered if she was always aware of them, as if they had an unseen presence on her human form.

Retelling their magical visions made them uneasy, and the group shivered in unison, drawing closer to the fire.

"How long do you think this will take?" Beansprout asked.

Fahey still seemed caught in the tendrils of his dreamlike trance, gazing out at the mist as if hoping to penetrate its secrets. He murmured, "It could take weeks. We have no idea of what Tom has to do or where he must go. I wish I was with him."

Woodsmoke frowned. "Or it could take just hours. He might be back here before nightfall."

"I'm sure it will take longer than one night, Woodsmoke," Brenna suggested. "We may as well make ourselves comfortable. We should start cooking." She stood up and rolled her shoulders. "I'm going to see what else is happening out there." She nodded across the moor. "I'll see you later." In a blink she had gone, soaring upwards until she was only a black speck.

Woodsmoke laughed dryly. "I guess that means I should cook."

"We'll help," Jack said, volunteering himself and Fahey.

Beansprout left them to it, and headed to the standing stones. They fascinated her, and she walked around them, her fingers tracing the carvings, feeling the warmth of the stone against her palm. *How long had they stood here, unchanged by the wind, rain, and burning sun? Who had made them?* It must have taken a long time to carve these beautiful shapes and figures, with their detailed expressions of fear, wonder, and horror. She recognised some of the creatures from the carvings they had seen on the gateways, and in the great cavern in the Realm of Water, but others were strange and unnerving: creatures with tentacles, multiple limbs, large eyes, pointed teeth, snarling expressions, and sharp claws. She should have been frightened, but instead felt wonder at being in such a place; that such a place could even exist. Beansprout felt suspended at the edge of the world, hovering between the known of her past and the unknown of her future. She had moved from one set of expectations to another, and should have been scared at this uncertainty, but felt only excitement.

She looked over to where her grandfather stood talking to Fahey, gestures filling the space between them, and understood why he would want to stay here. The limits of his life had shifted dramatically. His best friend was a bard, a dreamer and spinner of magic. His words conjured worlds and images, desires and hopes; they chased away the old normality, replacing it with breath-taking strangeness and wonder. In fact, this whole place was a breath-taking wonder.

Beansprout realised she didn't care how long they had to wait for Tom. It didn't seem to matter anymore. The important thing was being here, to witness whatever happened. She wondered if this was the spell the Lady of the Lake had cast upon her, but then admitted to herself that this feeling had been growing for some time; it had just taken until now to recognise it.

It felt like a lifetime had passed since they had crossed through the portal. She had no idea what was happening at home, and wasn't sure that she really cared. Hopefully, no one was frantic with worry. Perhaps their absence hadn't been noticed; maybe some mysterious magic had taken care of that. She nodded to herself. *Yes, that would be for the best.*

She looked up to watch Brenna high above, a speck against the grey sky. *A bird-shifter. How amazing was that? There must be more of her kind, but where were they, and why was she living with Woodsmoke's family?* She remembered Brenna's awkwardness sometimes, her reluctance to share too much, and the worried looks that passed between her and Woodsmoke. She had a feeling that it was something to do with this mysterious Queen, but she was reluctant to pry.

Suddenly, Brenna swerved overhead, pulling out of her lazy swooping circles, heading back to where they had come from. *What had she seen to make her move so quickly?* Beansprout turned to watch her progress, but she disappeared from sight. She watched anxiously for a few more minutes, relieved to see her finally return and land next to the camp where the others were gathered around the fire in the thickening dusk, and she ran to join them.

"Prince Finnlugh is coming, with a small retinue of guards," Brenna announced.

Woodsmoke was so shocked that he stood up and looked back over the moor. "What? How close are they? How big is the guard?"

"About two dozen. The Duchess of Cloy was with him, too. At present, they are only at the edge of the moor, but they travel far quicker than we do and will be here in another day or so."

"Herne's horns! What does he want? It can't be good!"

"Not necessarily," Fahey said. "They may be here to help. Historically, they're not fans of the Queen."

"And Tom did invite him," Brenna reminded them.

"I don't trust them," Woodsmoke said, "but there's really not much we can do against so many, is there?" He sighed with exasperation. "I suppose a day gives us a little time, let's hope it's longer, and Tom will be back by then."

"Even so, we can't outrun them," Brenna pointed out, settling by the fire to warm her hands. "We just have to wait and be ready for whatever happens. I'll take first watch later, but hopefully it will be an uneventful night."

Beansprout was still standing, watching the inky darkness spread across the moor, and she couldn't help but feel a thrill of excitement at the prospect of meeting Prince Finnlugh and his retinue.

# Chapter 13: Arthur's Icy Tomb

Tom's torch was still burning strongly and he had no idea what time it was, but his stomach grumbled loudly. He paused on one of the steps, drank some water, and ate a few biscuits.

Other than the torchlight that flickered in the occasional draughts that eddied around him, Tom was surrounded by a musty blackness. He had passed passageways that branched off from broad landings, but as instructed, he kept to the main path, heading ever deeper into the earth. Heaviness settled upon him, and he truly felt the weighty expectation of his strange inheritance. He pulled his sleeve up to look at his birthmark.

It seemed to move in the torchlight, and he ran his fingers over it as if he might feel its edges raised, different from his normal skin. But it felt the same as usual. He hadn't really taken notice of it before, and to him its darker tone didn't even look like a sword.

He sighed, gathered his things, and started down the path again.

Tom hadn't gone far when he heard voices—vague whisperings and murmurs, and he froze, straining to hear where they were coming from. But it was impossible; they seemed everywhere and nowhere at the same time. He swallowed his fear and resisted the urge to run back to the cave, and instead carried on, deciding they were a trick of his ears and the pressing darkness. Eventually, he came across a tiny, yellow light in a passage off to his right, the entrance marked by a metal gate on rusty hinges. As he paused before it, the gate swung wide in welcome. The yellow light at the end of the passage flared brightly, and blossom-scented air raced out to envelop him. It looked so welcoming and warm, and he was so cold that he decided to investigate. He stepped closer and the light flared even brighter, but as he laid his hand on the gate, his own torch flickered and nearly went out, causing him to halt sharply. He stepped back warily as Vivian's warning came back to him—stay on the path. A shriek pierced the silence and the light at the end of the passage disappeared, and in its absence he saw glowing red eyes and smelled rotten flesh. Tom fled downwards, sick with fear, cursing his stupidity and almost stumbling over his own feet. Taking deep breaths, he noticed his torch was once again burning strong and bright, and he vowed he wouldn't forget Vivian's instructions a second time.

As Tom plunged deeper underground it became colder and colder, and by the time he reached the bottom of the steps, his breath appeared as icy clouds. There was now only one route to follow: a passageway, thick with frost that disappeared into intense darkness. Feeling he was nearing his goal, Tom set off quickly, anxious to be out of this horrible place. What had Vivian said Avalon was? A place where things begin, end, rest, wait, and watch. What the hell did that mean? She was infuriatingly cryptic.

Finally, his extremities almost frozen, Tom saw a dim light ahead, and emerged into a long cavern with a low roof that seemed to be made of crystal. Murky green light was filtering through it, and a flash of movement overhead made him realise that he was now under the lake. It was like being in an aquarium.

He turned his attention to the rest of the cavern, noting that the floor was made of flat slabs of stone, the walls were hewn from rock, and the entire place was covered in thick, frozen vines. More importantly, in the centre of the space, partly obscured by the tangle of leaves, was a rectangular tomb made of opaque crystal, like the roof, and deep within it he could see the shadowy shape of a man.

The tomb of King Arthur.

Tom sighed with relief and yelled, "Yes!" He'd made it. Now, he just needed to work out what to do. If King Arthur wasn't dead, why was he in a tomb? Bloody Vivian. Couldn't she have been a bit more direct?

He wedged his torch into a break in the rock, then squared up to the tomb, braced himself, and tried to push the lid off. Nothing happened, and he swore loudly and profusely, enjoying the fact that no one could tell him off for his profanities. But it was at this point he realised, as he blew on his hands in an effort to warm them up, that the tomb wasn't made of some kind of crystal. It was formed from ice. There was actually no lid; the entire thing was one, solid block.

How the hell was he supposed to open it? The sharpest thing he had in his pack was his pocketknife. What he needed was a pick-axe. He dropped his pack on the floor, pulling out everything in an effort to find something useful, when he saw the silver branch—or bough, as Fahey had called it. Did he need to use it here? Vivian had said it would help.

Its silvery brightness glowed in the dim green light, and with fumbling fingers, Tom pulled it out. He walked around the cavern peering at the vines, hoping the branch in his hand would fit somewhere, but nothing looked suitable.

It was at this point his adrenalin ran out and he slumped to the floor, repacking his bag as he sat staring at the tomb and the sleeping King within it. Something glinted in King Arthur's hands, something that ran the length of his body. Curiosity overcame his tiredness, and he stood and leaned over the tomb, peering within its depths, and grinned as he realised it was Excalibur. He shook his head in disbelief. He was actually looking at King Arthur and his famous sword. *How weird was this?*

Tom put the silver branch down on the tomb and pulled the water from his pack. There was hardly any left, and he might need to share it, assuming he could somehow wake the King. They would have to climb all the way out again. *What if the King was old and decrepit? Or severely weakened, after sleeping for hundreds of years?*

He stared absently down, mulling over what to do, when he noticed that the contact with the tomb seemed to be doing something to the silver branch. Its brightness was decreasing, and it was turning back into wood, as it had been when Vivian gave it to him. New shoots were sprouting rapidly, and tendrils spread across the tomb. As they touched the old frozen vines, they started thawing and growing too with alarming speed.

Tom leapt backwards as the vines spread, threatening to entangle his feet, and the walls started moving with green, wriggling growth. Within seconds the tomb was invisible under a mass of vines, and the bough returned to silver, glinting under the fresh leaves. An ominous rumbling dragged his attention back to the entrance, and he saw with a shock that the new growth had smothered it completely, its weight collapsing the roof in that section.

He was trapped.

In front of him, thick shoots were now punching their way through the tomb's weakening ice. The cavern walls began to drip with moisture as the temperature warmed. Chunks of the icy tomb fell to the floor, and puddles formed beneath his feet. Tom pocketed the Silver Bough, put his backpack on, and began to pull chunks of ice away in an effort to speed things up.

A movement in the wall opposite stopped him momentarily. He felt a breeze and heard a dull roar. What now? He looked warily at the wall, and felt a splash of icy water on his head. Then he saw drops hitting the floor across the cavern. He looked up with horror. The roof wasn't made of crystal. It was made of ice, too—and it was melting. He would drown if he didn't get out of there quickly.

Tom grabbed the torch, ran to the wall, and pushed aside the vines. Thrusting the torch forward, he saw another long passageway, and he could hear running water.

Something slid and crashed behind him, and he heard a groan. His heart in his mouth, he spun around and saw King Arthur roll free of the ice. The King rose onto his hands and knees, breathing deeply, and then with great effort, he slowly stood up. Excalibur lay at his feet.

He was younger than Tom had expected, and taller, with a powerful build. He had shoulder-length dark hair, a short beard, and he wore finely stitched linen and leather clothing. For a few seconds he looked dazed, but then he focused on Tom, saying something that Tom couldn't understand.

Tom shook his head. "What? I'm sorry; I can't understand you. Look, we're under the lake, and we have to go. Now!" Tom grabbed King Arthur by the arm and pulled him towards the exit.

He resisted, again saying something else that Tom couldn't understand.

Tom pointed upwards at the dripping roof, trying to show the urgency of their situation. "We have to go—*now!*" He pulled on King Arthur's arm again.

King Arthur looked up and around the cavern, and then understanding apparently dawned. He sheathed his sword and staggered after Tom, who headed through the gap and set off quickly along the tunnel.

As Tom ran, he glanced behind him, but King Arthur kept up. The passageway led to an underground river and then turned sharply left, and Tom skidded to a halt, narrowly avoiding falling into the swiftly flowing, inky black water and certain death. The noise of running water was deafening. Tom glanced back and saw that King Arthur was right behind him, so he set off again. The path began to rise upwards, and the roar of water became louder until they reached a steep, crumbling rock face. To their right, a waterfall tumbled over the rocks, its spray filling the air around them.

Tom peered upwards into the darkness, and wondered how high they would have to climb. It was impossible to see where it ended. He gripped the torch tightly, and with his other hand he sought hand-holds as he clambered up the treacherous path. If he dropped the torch, they would be in total blackness. King Arthur slipped and muttered behind him.

Tom had the horrible feeling that the entire journey back to the surface was going to be this difficult, and they were a very long way down. If the cavern roof cracked it would flood, as would the path they were on. He did not want to drown. Don't think of anything, just keep climbing, step by step. His limbs burned, his fingers were sore and bruised, and his chest ached with every breath he took. Beyond his laboured breathing and the roar of the waterfall, Tom heard and felt a deeper rumble. Was that the roof collapsing?

Just when he thought he couldn't climb any longer, the path started to level out and the roof came into view not far above his head. He collapsed onto the ground, gasping for breath, closely followed by the King who lay next to him, chest heaving.

Tom wondered why King Arthur couldn't understand him; it would make things tricky. And then it struck him— Vivian had said to use the branch. He pulled it out of his pocket and, nudging King Arthur with his foot, handed it to him. He sat up, looking puzzled. "Why are you giving me this?"

Tom grinned and sat up, too. "Yes! I can understand you now! It worked."

King Arthur looked shocked, and then smiled. "What an interesting trick!" He turned the bough over and over in his hands, as if it would reveal its secrets, then handed it back to Tom, looking at him intently. "To whom do I owe my life?"

"I'm Tom, and I was sent by Vivian to wake you. She needs you." He held his hand out, and King Arthur shook it. He added hesitantly, "It's an honour to meet you, King Arthur. Should I bow?"

He laughed. "Absolutely not, and please, call me Arthur. Thank you for rescuing me, I think. Where on Earth are we?"

"Under the lake that surrounds Avalon, and we better get a move on. I think I heard that roof collapse."

Arthur nodded, and then pointed behind Tom. "Good idea. I can see a boat, so let us use that, because I'm not sure my legs can keep going much longer."

Tom saw Arthur was right. They were on the edge of water—not a river, though. Something bigger. He could feel a change in the air and in the noise around them. The far side was hidden in darkness, but there was a small boat pulled up onto the shore, away from the racing water that plunged over the edge.

They pushed the boat into the water and clambered in, bobbing unevenly as they sat on narrow benches. Tom propped the torch in the bow as they looked for ways to move the boat, but within seconds, the boat started to move on its own.

Arthur murmured, "Vivian is always resourceful."

Tom snorted. "That's one way of putting it."

"And where are we now? Other than under the lake." He looked wary, as if he knew Tom was about to tell him something odd.

Tom watched him, curious as to how he would take the news. "Well, we're not in England anymore. We are in The Otherworld, The Land of the Fey, the Realm of Earth, or something of the sort."

Arthur nodded slowly, but his gaze turned inward. "Ah! Merlin's deal. I didn't really believe that. I should have known better." He focused sharply. "How long has it been?"

"Since your sort-of death? About 1,500 hundred years or so."

Arthur's mouth fell open in shock. "So long? By the Gods, that's—" He stuttered for a moment. "That's unbelievable. But Vivian is still alive?"

"She is."

His eyes widened. "Anyone else? Gawain? Bedevere?"

"I don't think so." Tom shook his head sadly. He wondered whether to tell him that he was his descendent, but it seemed the wrong time, somehow. Arthur needed to come to terms with the news.

"So, I'm alone." Arthur nodded with grim acceptance, then lay down, eyes closed, his head on the edge of the boat, feet tucked under the bench.

Tom watched him for a moment, and guessed he was in his thirties. He looked fit, as if he'd been asleep for hours rather than centuries. His sword lay sheathed at his side, and the hilt's strange engravings flashed in the light. Had he only been this old when he'd died? Or had the magical sleep made him younger?

Tom looked again at his birthmark, comparing it to the sword next to Arthur. Was it his imagination, or did his birthmark look sharper than before, like an actual sword? Were there shapes coiling in its centre? He shook his head as if to free himself from a trance, covered his arm, and shivered.

The boat moved silently across the inky black depths of the lake, the roof low and uneven over their heads. They had come such a long way that Tom guessed they were travelling back to the lakeshore, not the Isle of Avalon. He glanced up, unsettled that there was water above them and below, with the possibility of more water arriving. If this cavern flooded, the water level would start to rise, and there wasn't much room for that.

Without warning, they plunged into mist. Mist underground? Faerie magic strikes again. Tom was exhausted. He lay down in the bottom of the boat and gazed at the roof passing overhead, trusting that Vivian would protect them.

# Chapter 14: Waiting and Watching

The group at the lakeside woke later than usual, but it was still earlier than Beansprout would ever rise at home. The first thing she did after waking was feel her arm, where the spear had punctured it. It was healing quickly now, and had begun to itch. It would surely leave a scar. She smiled; she had a battle wound.

As she rolled onto her back, Beansprout saw the blue sky above her, pale like a duck egg. Eager to start the day, she sat up, clutching the blanket around her shoulders, and faced the wall of mist stretched across the lake. Her grandfather and Fahey were still dozing, but someone had added wood to the fire, and it blazed brightly. A kettle hung above it, steam seeping from its spout. She smiled with contentment. She could get used to this. It was so freeing to be lying on the lakeshore beside a fire. She felt she could do anything, go anywhere. Anything she needed, she had with her.

Before they'd gone to sleep last night, Fahey had told them one of his stories—to help them relax, he'd said. He told a tale about an ancient king who outwitted a forest goblin. It was very funny, particularly as he paced around the fire, acting out the parts. Beansprout presumed he was trying to make them feel brave, and it sort of worked.

She grabbed her dirty cup from beside her and walked over to the lake to swill it, before refilling it with sweet herb tea. Sitting down again she looked around for Brenna and Woodsmoke. She presumed Brenna was flying, but where was Woodsmoke? She swivelled to look back over the moor. Grasses and heathers rippled all the way to the horizon, a blackish-green line where the wood began. To the north the Old Forest, otherwise known as Aeriken Forest. She rolled the name around her tongue, and tried to imagine what mysteries it contained. Woodsmoke had told her it was the home and hunting grounds of the Aerikeen, and that some of the Realm of the Earth's stranger creatures lived there.

Although there was no sign of Prince Finnlugh approaching, a figure bobbed over to the left. It was Woodsmoke, emerging from one of the hollows.

"I think we should move," he said as he sat down next to her. "The hollow over there is broad and deep, sheltered from the wind, and more importantly will give us cover from unwelcome attention."

"Do you really think we're in danger?"

"I don't know, but I'd rather we at least try and hide."

"Wouldn't we be better off heading back to the Tor? At least then we'd be high, and able to defend ourselves."

Woodsmoke shook his head. "It would take too long. And what if Tom arrives back here and finds he's alone, without help?"

"He'd better not be on his own!" Beansprout said, frowning.

"Even if he's with the King, we can't leave him here."

"No, I know. It was just a suggestion. But, what if they surround us—around the hollow?" Beansprout was excited about meeting Prince Finnlugh, but the closer he became, the more nervous she was.

"They're more likely to head for the shore. We can retreat back across the moor."

"But you said they're too fast!"

He looked at her, exasperated. "Stop being argumentative. We're in a very difficult situation!"

"Sorry." She looked sheepish. "Just trying to help."

"If you two have finished bickering, I would like to agree with Woodsmoke," Jack said, stirring from his blankets. "Let's head for the hollow. I feel a bit exposed here."

They ate breakfast and then packed up, quickly setting up camp in their new spot. Brenna returned at midday and joined them around the fire.

"The Prince and his company are nearly halfway across the moor," she told them as she helped herself to a drink.

Beansprout gasped. "They move so quickly! It took us days to travel that far."

"They have a far greater magic than we ever will," Woodsmoke said, "and their horses are swifter and more powerful. They're bred from an ancient line of magical beasts."

"It is said that one of the royal line came with his followers to this lakeshore, millennia ago, to raise a new house," Fahey said thoughtfully. "He wanted to solve the mystery of the lake and reach the Isle of Avalon. But not even he was strong enough to do that."

"Why, what happened to him?" Jack asked.

"He disappeared and was never seen again. His cries echoed through the halls day and night, and many perished trying to find him. They abandoned the place in the end. No one could stand it there."

"Where was it?"

He nodded downwards. "Somewhere beneath our feet!"

Beansprout looked uncomfortably at the ground below them.

Brenna downed her tea, and stood up. "I'm going to remain out there, as a bird, perched on the standing stones. I can keep watch for them—and for Tom." She flitted out of the hollow, not waiting for a response.

"I've changed my mind," grumbled Fahey. "I don't like hiding here. It makes me feel like a coward. And I can't see what's going on."

Woodsmoke gave him a long, impatient look. "We are not hiding like cowards! We are trying to protect ourselves from attack, old man. Are you going to produce a sword from under that cloak?"

He bristled with resentment. "That's unfair and you know it."

"Apart from your skill with words, have you anything that could protect us?"

"I might know a few charms that could make us invisible, a protection from unwanted eyes." He looked sly, as if he was doing things he shouldn't.

"Good, do it."

The light was falling and long shadows stretched over the ground when Brenna returned. They were sitting at the base of the hollow, a bright fire burning merrily, eating a supper of stewed rabbit that filled the air with a rich, warm smell, and Beansprout reflected on what a good idea it had been to move. It was so much warmer out of the moorland wind, and it felt safer somehow.

Fahey filled a bowl with food and passed it to Brenna, asking, "What's the news?"

"Not much. Apart from Prince Finnlugh's advance, nothing else is going on out there."

Woodsmoke sighed. "I don't think Tom will appear tonight. I had hoped we'd be out of here before Prince Finnlugh arrived, but now…"

"I just hope he's safe," Jack said, worry etched across his face.

Beansprout adjusted the blanket across her shoulders and, turning to Fahey, said, "Maybe to pass the time and stop us from worrying, you should tell us another tale."

He smiled. "I have many. Any particular one?"

"Yes. I would like to know more about King Arthur."

"There are many such tales. King Arthur's knights, King Arthur's battles, King Arthur and Merlin…"

"I'd just like to know a little bit about *him*."

"Then I shall keep it simple. Centuries ago, Britain was in turmoil. There were many kings, fighting for power and land, and then outsiders came who fought them all. One king, Uther, was more powerful than most, and he had a very clever man as his advisor. He was called Merlin.

"There were rumours that Merlin was a wizard. They said he could control the elements—earth, water, air, and fire; that he could turn night to day, control animals, and cross to the Otherworld. At that time, the paths between both worlds were easier to walk, if you knew where to look. Many fey and humans passed to and fro, and Merlin crossed many times.

"King Uther had a son, called Arthur. He was born in Tintagel, King Uther's castle by the sea. Merlin spent much time with him, teaching him many things. The things he couldn't teach, he made sure Arthur learnt from other skilled men.

"Arthur grew strong, and yet he was a gentle man, keen

to talk with his enemies rather than fight. But when he did fight, everyone marvelled at his strong hands and quick feet, and warriors admired his skill and pledged him allegiance.

"When King Uther died, Arthur became king, but the time was fraught with danger. In spite of the outsiders who continued to invade, the other kings still fought each other ferociously. Merlin wanted to give Arthur a sword with magical powers to protect him in battle, and it would also unite the people, allowing them to vanquish their enemies. He crossed through the mists to the Otherworld to bargain for such a weapon.

"His friend, Vivian, had great influence amongst the fey. She was wise with arcane knowledge and power, and she lived upon the Isle of Avalon that straddled both worlds. She agreed to speak to the Forger of Light, and after a negotiation, he consented to make a sword—Excalibur. But in exchange for this magical weapon, Vivian demanded that Arthur come to the Otherworld when his life was all but over, to rest until he was needed. Merlin felt he had little choice and agreed to the bargain, though he never forgave Vivian for it.

"So, Merlin performed one of his greatest feats of magic. In order to prove the sword's powers, and Arthur's power to rule over all, he set the sword in a great stone, telling the kings that whoever could withdraw the sword would be the one and only true King of Britain. Many tried and many failed, all except Arthur. He withdrew the sword from the stone as if he were pulling it from butter. He held it aloft, and the sun struck it and dazzled all those watching. They fell at his feet, acknowledging that he was the one, true King.

"These warriors became his knights, and to promote fairness and equality, King Arthur had them sit at a round table, and the land of Britain united to fight and repel the newcomers. His court was at Camelot, and it dazzled beneath the sun and moon like a shining jewel. King Arthur ruled for years and years. His knights fought, quested, feasted, and held tournaments. His people loved him, and the land was at peace.

"But even in the land of light, some still sought the shadows.

"King Arthur had an older half-sister, called Morgan le Fay. She resented the time that Merlin gave to King Arthur, and she begrudged the King's success. Morgan was half-fey and half-human, and a powerful sorceress. Merlin didn't trust her. She conspired against King Arthur, seeking to destroy him. Using her magical arts, she lured King Arthur's nephew, Mordred, with promises of power and wealth. She filled his head with lies and trained him to kill King Arthur. She was patient, waiting and watching until the King was distracted. Finally, the time came.

"King Arthur was betrayed by his wife, Queen Guinevere. She was beautiful but weak, and desired Sir Lancelot, one of King Arthur's greatest knights. And Lancelot desired her. When King Arthur found out, Queen Guinevere was banished, and Lancelot fled the kingdom, swiftly pursued by King Arthur, who chased him far and wide, full of anger and vengeance.

"Morgan seized her chance. By the time King Arthur returned, Mordred had taken the land. They fought in the great Battle of Camlann, and King Arthur was mortally wounded. As required by the bargain, the King's body was carried to the lakeshore from whence he could be taken to Avalon. Excalibur was thrown into the lake as a signal to Vivian, and she emerged from the mists with her eight sister-priestesses to escort King Arthur to the Otherworld.

"And Britain fell into darkness."

Fahey was solemn, and turned to the fire. Beansprout followed his gaze. She stared into the flames, remembering Vivian and the large boat with the dragon-headed prow coming to take Tom to wake the King, and wondered if it was the same boat that had taken King Arthur to Avalon.

# Chapter: 15 Strange Alliances

Tom daydreamed as the unbelievable reality of his situation nagged at his brain. He lay on his back and gazed up at the thick tendrils of mist obscuring his view. Again he had the feeling of not moving, of being suspended in time and place, caught forever in a pocket of air between two lakes.

King Arthur was motionless beside him. Tom couldn't understand how a man who had slept for hundreds of years could want to sleep again so soon. Feeling charitable, he put it down to physical exhaustion. It had been an abrupt awakening, after all. Finding yourself on the floor of an underground cavern after being asleep, in ice, for hundreds of years, would be very odd. He wondered if Arthur could remember dying? He would ask him when he woke up.

Tom wanted to sit up and look around, but the mist continued to hide the low roof and he didn't want to hit his head. He remained where he was, bored, and feeling as if he had been in the dark forever. He lost track of time, drifting in and out of a light sleep until he heard a distant shout. He thought his ears were playing tricks, but then he heard it again, getting closer. His skin prickled with goose bumps and he froze as he became fully alert. *Something was coming towards them.* Again he heard a loud moan, and then a splash. He rolled onto his stomach and peered over the edge of the boat, dreading that he might see something there, but all was dark except for the small sphere of his torchlight on mist and water. He hurriedly lay down again and the sound stopped. With a sudden rush of emotion, he wanted to see the sky again and feel a warm breeze. When he got out of here, maybe it was time to go home.

Eventually, a soft light banished the darkness and the mist disappeared, revealing a high, domed rocky roof. Tom sat up and peered into the gloom. They were again on a river, but to their right was a large antechamber made from golden stone. Huge columns reached up to a vaulted roof, and at the rear were enormous double doors.

Tom nudged Arthur. "Wake up, look at this."

Arthur barely stirred, but Tom kept prodding him with his foot, unable to take his eyes from what looked like the entrance to a palace. The boat changed course, headed to the riverbank, and stopped.

Arthur sat up, bleary-eyed. He looked as amazed as Tom. "Where are we?"

"I've no idea, but I think this is how we find a way out."

They clambered out onto shallow stone steps and walked to the ornate doors, decorated with rose gold. Arthur cocked a raised eyebrow at Tom. "After me."

He pushed open one of the doors and it swung silently back, revealing a hallway that glowed with pale light. There was no obvious source of the light, except perhaps from the stone itself, but it was clearly the entrance to a large building. They stepped inside, and their footsteps echoed around them.

"Wow!" Tom said, staring with amazement.

"Indeed." Arthur nodded, his eyes alive with curiosity. "Well Tom, I have no idea where we're going, but we better get on with it."

Arthur carried his sword in readiness, even though there was no sign of life around them, and set off at a quick pace. Tom carried the torch—just in case darkness fell once more—and followed Arthur ever deeper into a labyrinth of rooms and corridors. He thought this was possibly the weirdest place he'd been so far. It was creepy, because it was so obviously deserted. But someone had lived here; someone had built all of this. *But who?*

A long, wailing cry echoed in the air, and Arthur halted in alarm, looking around with his sword raised. "What was that?"

"I heard that earlier, on the lake," Tom said, turning slowly and seeing nothing but a deserted passageway. "But I couldn't see anything then, either. Let's get out of here, quickly! We must still be deep beneath the earth, so we need stairs."

Another wail punctuated the silence, and it spurred them on, frantically trying to find some way of getting to the surface.

They had just entered another large room with dusty rugs and ornate furniture, when Arthur said, "Tom."

"Yes," he answered impatiently, already heading for the door on the far side.

"Look behind us."

Tom saw water lapping gently across the floor through the door they just entered. "Crap! The cave's roof must have collapsed. The cavern is flooding!"

"Vivian doesn't like to make life too easy, does she?" Arthur muttered angrily.

They ran along corridors and sloshed through rooms while the water continued to rise, until eventually they came to a broad set of stone stairs ascending to another level.

"Yes!" Tom exclaimed. "This will buy us some time."

On the next level, they saw rooms stretching away on either side, but no other stairs, and they raced down more corridors, doubling back on themselves several times when they came to dead ends, until they came to a large room with stairs running both up and down in the centre. Without even stopping to discuss it, they both raced upwards and came to a sealed, circular space.

Arthur turned quickly. "There are no doors here."

"There has to be some way out," Tom reasoned, "or else what was the point of stairs leading up here? Start looking."

They examined the walls closely, feeling along the cracks in the stonework and wood panelling, hoping to find a hidden opening or some sort of mechanism, but with no success.

"Let's try the floor, Tom," Arthur finally said. "Look, there's an interesting pattern right in the middle."

He was right. The floor had an intricate tiled surface, and at its centre was a swirling design. Arthur dropped to his knees and pressed on the central stone. With a rumble and a grating sound that set Tom's teeth on edge, stones started to rise around them.

Arthur looked at him and grinned. "Exactly as I thought."

The floor formed itself into a series of steps that joined up with steps descending from above. Blue sky winked through an opening in the roof, and Tom sighed with relief. Neither of them could get up the stairs fast enough.

They emerged in the centre of the standing stones, as the sun was dropping towards the horizon and the stones' shadows fell long and dark across the moor. Brenna stood at the edge of the circle, grinning broadly, while Woodsmoke,

Beansprout, Fahey, and Jack raced over, almost colliding with her. Woodsmoke paused, looking relieved, while Beansprout and Jack rushed to Tom's side. Fahey, although pleased, looked far more interested in the gaping hole beneath them.

"Tom, you're back! You did it!" Jack whooped, grabbing Tom in a bear hug.

Tom grinned broadly. "I guess I did. Let me introduce you to King Arthur."

Arthur had been waiting quietly, but now he stepped forward, greeting them each in turn, and repeating what he'd said to Tom. "Please, do not address me as King, Arthur will do just fine!" Beansprout blushed as Arthur took her hand and kissed it, and Tom watched as Arthur and Woodsmoke assessed one another carefully.

*The myth had become a man, but what kind of man was he?*

As they shook hands, Tom glanced across the moor, puzzled. "Who's that?"

They all turned as the setting sun fell on the approaching Prince and his group; their silver armour flashed, the horses' black coats gleamed, and their pennants fluttered in the wind as they raced towards them.

"Prince Finnlugh, and a few friends…" Brenna explained, her eyebrows raised and a smile playing across her lips.

"He *came*?" Tom wasn't sure whether to be pleased or appalled.

"So much for trying to hide," Woodsmoke groaned.

Fahey looked at the hole, then at Tom. "So where did you come from, Tom?"

"You won't believe what's down there!"

Fahey smirked. "I bet I will."

Woodsmoke ignored them all and walked to the edge of

the standing stones, Brenna at his side, watching the approaching riders. The Prince and his party arrived in a swirl of wind and thundering hooves, and in one swift movement, the Prince pulled his horse to a stop, jumped down, and strode towards Tom and Arthur. Before he could get close, however, Woodsmoke stopped him, stepping directly into his path.

"What do you want here, Prince Finnlugh?"

"I was invited," he replied, looking past Woodsmoke towards Brenna and Tom, his eyes finally coming to rest on Arthur and the glinting steel of Excalibur, which was still in his hand. "I wanted to know if it was true." He met Woodsmoke's steady gaze. "I'm not here to cause trouble."

Woodsmoke glanced at Brenna, who nodded, and then moving aside, said, "Then you are welcome."

Prince Finnlugh advanced on Arthur, and then swept to the floor with a regal bow. "King Arthur, I am Prince Finnlugh, Bringer of Starfall and Chaos, Head of the House of Evernight. These are auspicious times."

Arthur bowed his head, wariness behind his eyes. "Arthur Pendragon, King of Britain, Boar of Kernow, the overlord of Wales, Cornwall, and the North. To what do I owe this pleasure?"

Tom smiled to himself. It seemed there were occasions when Arthur liked his title.

Prince Finnlugh gave him a tight smile. "I believe we have much to discuss, but let us sit first and celebrate your return." He gestured behind him, where his men were already setting up camp.

Tom looked at Woodsmoke's wry smile and returned it with his own.

*So that's how you introduce yourself to a King.*

It was a strange company that gathered that night on the edge of the moor, the brooding wall of mist on the lake marking the edge of the visible world. Several campfires had been lit, and the Prince and the Duchess had magically erected enormous pavilions for shelter, grown from the heathers and small bushes that lay thickly around them.

Before darkness had fallen, Fahey and several of the Prince's party had been unable to resist descending the great stone steps leading to the underground palace. Not that they could explore far—the water continued to rise, and the lower floor was now completely submerged.

Tom lounged on a couch in one of Prince Finnlugh's pavilions, revelling in his moment of glory. He tried to work out how deep he had been and how far he'd travelled, but time and distance had lost all meaning. He was amazed to find that only two days had passed—it felt more like a week. He looked across to where Arthur sat by the fire, surrounded by people pressing him with questions. Fahey was gazing at him gleefully, unable to get enough of this unexpected figure from the past. Tom felt he should be more awed than he actually was, but he was so exhausted from the pace of the previous days that he couldn't properly take anything in. It was all too unreal.

Tom was more curious about the oddities of the Prince's party. The Duchess of Cloy had a towering mass of hair like an enormous wedding cake piled on her head. At least, he thought it was hair, but up close it actually looked like petals. She wore a pendant around her neck, on which hung a large, green stone mounted in gold—but the stone rested at the back of her neck, rather than at her throat. He was unnerved when it blinked like an eye, and even more unnerved when the Duchess turned around and gazed at him for long seconds. He could smell lilies, sweet and overpowering, and then as she turned away the smell vanished, leaving him feeling giddy and sick.

They were all odder than Woodsmoke, Brenna, and Fahey. He hadn't realised how much he'd grown used to his friends' otherness. But the people, or rather the fey, from the Royal Houses were very strange. Some had peach-like skin, soft and fuzzy, others had skin as smooth as silk, and a few were covered in whiskers. Their hair was soft, like balls of cotton candy, coloured like rainbows, or as white as snow. They were draped in magic; it crackled over them like static electricity.

Beansprout sat next to him. "You all right? You're very quiet."

"I'm exhausted. The rescuing business is hard work."

Tom had related earlier how he'd woken Arthur, and their mad dash through the tunnel and onto the underground lake. She laughed and looked to where Woodsmoke and the Prince sat next to the fire, speaking earnestly. "I think Woodsmoke is feeling happier about the Prince. I wonder what happens now?"

"Time to go back home, I guess," Tom said.

Beansprout took a deep breath. "I don't want to go back, Tom."

He sat up in shock. "*What?* Are you kidding me?"

"No. I love it here. I have room to think. I'm not going back, and you can't make me."

"You can't *not* go home! What would your mum say? She'd freak out."

Beansprout shrugged. "It's just the way I feel."

"You might feel it now, but you won't forever. What will you do here? You're being crazy. This isn't real," he said, gesturing at everything around them.

She looked at him as if he'd grown two heads. "Of course it's *real*. It's just a different reality."

"But you don't belong here."

"But I could," she said stubbornly. Getting up, she left him and walked towards Arthur. Sighing, and getting to his feet with difficulty because his leg muscles burned, Tom followed.

The Prince was gazing at Arthur's sword. It glinted in the firelight, which illuminated the rich and fantastical engravings along its polished blade and hilt. "Merlin was a powerful man to negotiate that for you, Arthur," he said admiringly.

Arthur laughed. "Merlin liked to get his own way, and generally did. Until his luck ran out." He sighed deeply, his laughter gone, and he gazed back to the fire. "It's because of that sword that I'm here, honouring his bargain, when I should be dust by now."

"You have a purpose, Arthur."

"It seems so. The Lady has decided that I must stop the Queen."

"And I must stop my brother. We can help each other."

"How?"

"Travel together, into Aeriken. I think they are working together... Why shouldn't we?"

Arthur looked at him, perplexed. "You don't need me. I don't have powerful magic."

"Neither do I, at the moment. I am weakened by the loss of my Jewel. But you have Excalibur. It is a talisman, forged by a powerful fey and full of protection. And besides, Vivian seems to think differently. She woke you especially for this reason. And I can help you!" Finnlugh's dark blue eyes fixed on Arthur with a persuasive intensity.

Woodsmoke and Brenna were watching this exchange with interest. *And no wonder*, thought Tom. A Prince who had isolated himself and his retinue in his Under-Palace for years, and an ancient King of Britain, far from home, brought back from the dead.

The Prince turned to them. "I'd like your help, too."

"How could I possibly help you?" asked Woodsmoke. "I have less magic than you, and I don't have an all-powerful sword."

"But you are a hunter and a tracker. If anyone can help find my brother, it should be you! And I bet you know Aeriken better than anyone here, except for perhaps…you, my dear." Finnlugh turned to Brenna. "You can fly, and therefore must be of the Aerikeen, ruled by our beloved, murderous Queen Gavina. You must want to stop her. She's hurting your people! Here's your chance," Finnlugh said in silky tones.

Brenna's face drained of colour at this revelation, and she looked at Woodsmoke, who nodded.

"All right," she said softly. "Let's make a plan."

# Chapter 16: Aeriken Forest

The trees of Aeriken Forest grew closely together, as if trying to repel newcomers. The thick green canopy was suffocating, and the forest interior was dim and dank. Worse than all of that, the track was narrow, forcing the band of travellers into a strung out, winding line.

The party had been travelling for several days now, but there was still no sign of the Duke of Craven. The deeper they moved into the forest, the more dangerous it became, and they had started to see wolves. Their howls echoed through the night, inciting fear and anxiety within them all.

Occasionally, a figure would materialise out of a tree trunk and stand watching from a distance, barely visible, dark-eyed and green-skinned, before melting back into the shadows. Fahey told them that they were dryads—spirits of the trees and guardians of the forest. The horses were spooked, skittering nervously in the darkness, and everyone was jumpy, thinking they were seeing things in the murky gloom.

They decided to track the sprites in the hope of imprisoning one and making him talk, and as twilight fell, Woodsmoke finally led them to an area the sprites had lived in. They halted, looking around with weapons drawn as they pulled into the deserted camp.

Arthur swore loudly. "They've obviously gone! Where now?"

Woodsmoke shook his head. "I'll try and find the trail tomorrow morning, but I haven't hunted here for years, and much has changed."

Brenna agreed. "It even feels different."

Finnlugh dismounted, sending his men to form a perimeter. "Well, we may as well stay here tonight. But I think we need to rethink our plan."

For a while they busied themselves making camp, and then when the fire was burning brightly and they all had food to eat, Beansprout sat next to Tom and said, "I think we're being watched."

He frowned as he chewed. "Why do you think that?"

"Can't you feel it? It's like there are a million eyes on us."

"It's just this place, the Otherworld. I feel like that all the time."

She shook her head. "No, this forest is different. It's brooding, wondering what we're doing here."

"Not surprising," Finnlugh said, overhearing her. He and the Duchess of Cloy were sitting around their fire, rather than with his guards. "We're blundering about like fools."

"So what do you propose?" Woodsmoke asked, looking at him in annoyance.

He turned to Brenna. "You need to lead us to the Aerie. A direct attack will be of more use now than this—" He flung his arm wide, disdainfully.

"This *was* your idea," Woodsmoke snapped.

Tom was confused. "What's the Aerie?"

"It's where the Queen lives, and the rest of my people," Brenna told him, her eyes dropping to the floor. "It's a palace built into the crags of a steep cliff, deep in the forest." She looked back at Finnlugh, her eyes narrowed. "But it's high up and she will have the advantage."

"My brother will be there—he must be!"

"You think he would risk the wrath of Gavina?"

"Of course my brother will risk it. He's desperate to use the Jewel, and he needs her to learn to wield it." Finnlugh looked troubled. "And once he does I fear he will be unstoppable. I have to find him."

"Why can't he use it now?" Tom asked. He'd wanted to ask this for days, but it had seemed inappropriate before now.

Finnlugh explained, "The Starlight Jewel belongs to the head of the House of Evernight—me. It responds to my will and enhances my natural power. At the moment, it won't work for him, but I know Queen Gavina has magic of her own. I'm worried she can manipulate its allegiance. I have to get to him as quickly as possible, and he must be with her. We have to go to the Aerie."

"What will we do once we get there?" Arthur asked, getting straight to the point. "You have guards, but several of our party are not fighters or trained in combat in any way. Travelling to the palace on a whim is foolhardy."

"Good question," Woodsmoke agreed. "Steal back the Jewel? Kill the Queen? Save her subjects and restore order to the forest?"

"I don't need sarcasm, thank you." Finnlugh turned to Arthur. "Do you have a better idea?"

"Not really." He shook his head thoughtfully. "I feel a little unprepared. Vivian seems to think that I shall know what to do, but frankly, I have no idea. I know nothing of this Queen, or what she is accused of. As you know, I have been in an enchanted sleep for a very long time. Perhaps someone can explain to me what it is she has done. Who is she?"

Brenna sighed a deep, bone-weary sigh that spoke of much despair and sorrow. "She walked out of the forest and into our palace hundreds of years ago. She was lost, hungry, exhausted, and needed help. I wasn't born then, but we all know the tale. She looked fragile and seemed kind, and quickly our King fell in love. His wife had died, and he was lonely.

"She wasn't one of us, but he didn't care, and neither did we. They were happy, and had children and then grandchildren. But as the years went on we began to see a different side to her. She was quick-tempered, manipulative, and sly, but the King couldn't see it because he was so in love. Then the King died and we mourned, and although his firstborn son should have become King, the Queen continued to rule.

"Slowly but surely things started to change for the worse, and when she was challenged, those who had dared to question her sovereignty started to disappear, particularly the heirs to the throne. And so I am sorry to say that her subjects left, drifting away to hidden parts of Aeriken where they could not be found. Some left the forest altogether, as I did.

"However, it seems she is now even worse. She has turned on even those whom she once trusted."

"But how did she gain so much control?" Arthur asked.

"She tricked us with her magic, until it was too late to stop her. This had never happened to us before…we were innocent and trusting. And if we couldn't stop her then, I'm not sure we can now. She seems to have gone mad, and power and madness are a frightening combination. And," she added, "the forest has changed, as well. There's no one here! It's as if all the forest creatures are hiding. Something is very wrong."

"Her whole court may be dead, if she has been 'hunting her own.'" Woodsmoke frowned. "I can see what Craven can gain from the Queen, but not what she can gain from him."

"I think she wants to steal the Starlight Jewel," Finnlugh said thoughtfully. "It could greatly increase her power."

"A double-cross?" Brenna sighed. "That would be her style."

"Well, in that case," Arthur said quietly, "we've wasted time. We must head to the palace at daybreak."

Tom stood at the base of a steep cliff gazing up at the summit, which was hidden by clouds and mist. His stomach lurched. It was insanely high up. But despite its height, it had been impossible to see on their approach, as the trees were so dense and the canopy so thick.

Their progress had been slow. Mosses covered the forest floor, disguising fallen trees, and the undergrowth was thick and tangled. It didn't help that the paths to the Aerie were hidden from outsiders, and Brenna had difficulty finding them again after so long.

The collective feeling of gloom had grown ever stronger, until they were barely sleeping, their dreams filled with strange images. They had taken their mind off things by practising their sword fighting skills with each other in the evenings. Beansprout and Tom were given swords suitable for learning with, and Arthur taught them, assisted by Finnlugh. Arthur and Finnlugh had sparred together, and they were frighteningly good. Both had pretended to be practising, but it was clear they each had a huge ego and couldn't wait to outplay the other.

For the past few days, wolves had stalked them, surrounding the camp at night. It had taken several volleys of arrows to make them retreat, their teeth flashing in the firelight, eyes glinting a frightening yellow. And then a group of dryads had appeared out of the shadows, silent and solemn, and those sitting around the fire had leapt to their feet, wondering how the dryads could have passed the guards. One stepped forward, asking the group, "What do you want here?"

Finnlugh answered, "The Queen and my brother. Nothing else."

"She will kill you. We hide from her now—*everyone* hides from her now. Beware your fire." And then they all vanished.

Finnlugh had put out the fire, and they had fallen silent in the dark.

A shout broke Tom's concentration, bringing him back to the present.

"Here! I've found the path!"

They had been looking for the narrow, stony path to the top for hours, and it seemed one of the guards had finally found it. His cry was faint, and Tom and Beansprout, who had been searching together, headed in his direction.

"At least we've found it," Beansprout said, as they fought their way through some tangled branches. "Are we going to go with them?"

"To the top?" he asked, frowning. "If they let us! I don't want to be left behind. Do you?"

"No!" She lowered her voice as she sidled closer, trying to keep her words from carrying to their granddad, who was close behind. "But what if they try to stop us?"

He slapped a branch out of the way. "We kick up a

fuss!"

When they reached the guard's side, another argument was already in full swing.

Prince Finnlugh was glaring at the Duchess of Cloy, who was glaring right back. "You should stay here and help protect the horses," he told her. "I can feel strong, strange magic. Something is very wrong here."

"I did not journey all this way to look after horses," she hissed in reply.

"If and when we escape from the palace, we'll need the horses to leave quickly. And I don't want anyone following us up that hill, either. I have no wish to be trapped." He smiled, widening his midnight blue eyes. "You are the only one I trust."

She rolled her eyes at him in a very un-Duchess like way. Tom found her difficult to read. She had said very little on their journey, preferring to watch and listen, and her silence was unnerving.

Jack joined in. "Actually, there's no way I can get up there without a horse. And there's certainly no way a horse can go up there! I'll stay, and so should you," he said to Tom and Beansprout.

"Not a chance," they answered at the same time.

"You have no idea how dangerous it may be!" argued Jack.

"And that's why I'm going," answered Tom. "I woke Arthur for this moment!"

"And don't think you'll change my mind, either!" Beansprout told him belligerently.

Fahey looked at Jack. "I'll stay. My knees will never manage that climb, unfortunately. And they're right. They should go. I feel they're part of this."

Jack looked as if he was going to protest, but then sighed and fell silent.

"See?" Finnlugh said to the Duchess. "You need to protect them, too."

She simmered with silent rage.

"You know I'm right, dear Duchess. You can feel it, too."

The eye in her pendant blinked slowly, and she stroked the necklace absentmindedly, as if listening to something. "All right. But if you're not back in three days, I shall leave you here."

"A deal, then. We start at first light."

They set their camp up under the trees, a short distance from the base of the crag, and the Prince and the Duchess magically built a tall fence of thick, thorny wood to protect them. The horses were secured inside, and the remaining guards positioned themselves around the edge.

The atmosphere was tense, with many of them continually glancing up at the rocky height they would have to scale the next day. Woodsmoke and Brenna conferred softly, while Arthur and Finnlugh had a robust discussion about how to proceed before settling their tension in a sword fight that became a little too aggressive. The Duchess, however, had settled in front of the small, bright fire. Rummaging in her bags, she brought out a variety of herbs that she cast into the flames, muttering quietly. With a sizzle, the flames changed colour to smoky blues and greens, and she sat for some time in a trance, gazing into their changing shapes. Eventually, she roused herself. "We shall manage without a fire again tonight."

"But the wolves—we need to keep them away!" Fahey said.

She turned her intense stare on him. "We must rely on the boundary. There are worse things than wolves out there. We must become invisible to all others, and we must appear dead if they come upon us."

"What? What's out there? And how can we appear dead?"

"We will smell dead, which will attract the wolves but keep away other things. Trust me on this, Fahey. You heard the dryads. We do not want the Queen finding us."

She started to prepare her magic, and Tom wondered yet again what he'd got himself into.

# Chapter 17: The Rotten Heart

The stony shale slid under Tom's feet, and he cursed as he climbed upwards. In some places, he even needed to bend double against the steepness of the path. He was grumpily aware of Brenna ahead of him, stepping lightly and effortlessly.

"Brenna, why aren't you flying?" he called.

She paused and looked back at him. "I can't."

He stopped in surprise, catching his breath and stretching out his aching back. "Why not?"

"Something's stopping me."

"Like what?"

"The magic Finnlugh mentioned. It's making the air feel syrupy, so I can't fly."

"It feels fine to me," Tom replied, puzzled.

Brenna had changed over the last few days. She had become wary and guarded, and her normal buoyancy had vanished. She called back over her shoulder, "Trust me, it's not."

Tom gazed out over the forest. He'd passed clefts and hollows, and forced his way through thick vegetation. They were far above the canopy now and Aeriken stretched to the horizon. His muscles burned with the effort, and he was sweaty and tired. The rest of the party toiled above him, all out of view. He sighed as Brenna disappeared too, then with a great effort he pushed on, muttering to himself about stupid quests.

A scream interrupted his thoughts and he looked up, pushing his hair out of his eyes. *Was that Beansprout?* The scream was followed by other shouts and yells. *Damn!* He ran, cursing his aching muscles. Rounding a corner, he stumbled into Brenna and the others.

Tom found himself on the edge of a wide cleft reaching deep into the cliff face. At its furthest corner were enormous gates hanging open, but the entrance was dark. The Aerie was beyond them, carved out of the rock. The cleft was filled with dead birds—hundreds of them. Their bodies lay thick upon the ground, bloodied, and their feathers torn. The smell of decay was strong, and Tom's stomach turned.

But that wasn't what had caused the shouts and screams. Spread on the cliffs above them, shackled to the rock, were scores more birds, and other creatures—some half-human, half-bird, their huge wings spread behind them. They were all dead. Many had rotted, leaving only skeletons to bleach in the sun.

Tears poured down Brenna's face, and the rest of them stood silently in shock.

"Who could have done this?" Arthur asked.

Nobody answered him.

Arthur pulled Excalibur from its scabbard. "Allow me." He pushed ahead and the rest of them followed, peering nervously upwards.

Their footsteps echoed on the rock, and shale slipped and slithered down with a threatening *hiss*. Woodsmoke halted briefly, his bow angled steeply upwards as he surveyed the escarpment. Apart from wind-ruffled feathers, nothing moved. He lowered his bow and walked on.

Beyond the shattered gates of the palace was a broad hall, illuminated by beams of light slanting in from the high roof—if it could be called a roof. Most of the walls were solid rock pitted with openings, out of which scrubby bushes and trees grew haphazardly, but closer to the top the walls became a latticework of rock, open to the wind and sky. Bridges of stone arched above them, weaving backwards and forwards, higher and higher, like the spokes of a wheel. It was eerily silent.

"It's like an aviary," the Prince murmured.

"Well, we *are* birds. What did you expect?" Brenna answered abruptly. Her tears had dried and she looked pale and angry.

Woodsmoke looked at Brenna, worry in his eyes. "Where is everyone? Surely they're not all dead."

"Hiding, I hope." Her voice trembled, and it was with a visible effort that she straightened her shoulders, taking deep breaths to steady herself.

Arthur scanned around. "Where to now?"

"I have no idea. I thought I'd see signs of my brother, but…" Finnlugh trailed off.

"We should go to the throne room," Brenna said. "That's where the Queen's power is concentrated. If he's anywhere, he'll be there."

Finnlugh asked, "Will she be there, too?"

Brenna shook her head. "I doubt it, or we'd have seen her by now. Or rather, she'd have seen us."

"Unless she's biding her time," Arthur said ominously.

An eerie cry punctuated the air and arrows winged through the air, catching them all by surprise. Some of Prince Finnlugh's guards were hit and fell awkwardly to the ground, instantly dead.

Brenna shouted, "This way!" and ran, zigzagging towards a room on the far side.

They raced after her. Woodsmoke and a few other guards fired arrows back at their attackers as they ran. A body almost fell on Tom, and he stumbled as he avoided it. Next to him, Beansprout sprinted, her hair streaming behind her. The guards who had already reached the doorway, fired arrows back into the hall.

Tom threw himself through the arch as Finnlugh shouted, "Keep behind me!"

The Prince muttered something unintelligible and thrust out his hand. A ball of white light flew into the hall and a *boom* echoed off the walls, hurting their ears. Several wood sprites thudded to the floor, clearly dead, their limbs splayed awkwardly.

"My brother is here!" Finnlugh declared with a wolfish grin. "Good. Lead on, Madame!"

Brenna pointed upwards. "The throne room is up there, right at the top."

"Up there?" Tom repeated, feeling his legs protesting already.

"There are steps cut into the rock on either side of the bridges," explained Brenna, "and rooms leading back into the hillside. But we have to cross the bridges to make our way up."

"And you can be sure there will be more sprites up there, too," Finnlugh added.

Tripping on each other's heels, they followed Brenna up the stone staircase until they reached the first bridge. Finnlugh's guards made their way quickly across first, and the rest jogged after them, weapons drawn. Thankfully the path was clear, and they were able to keep moving upwards.

Tom took deep breaths and tried not look down as he ran across the bridges, which were far too high and narrow for his liking. As they reached the end of each one, they paused to search for signs of life on the bridges above them and in the rooms on each level.

They halted their advance about a third of the way up to drink water and catch their breath, and Beansprout asked Brenna, "Did you live here?"

She nodded. "Yes, we all did from time to time. Although, most of the rooms are for those who serve the Royal Household. Like many shifters, we tend to live in human form more than our animal form, but it varies."

"So you served the household, too?" Arthur asked, puzzled. It was a good question. Brenna didn't have the demeanour of a household servant.

She was evasive. "I stayed here sometimes, but ultimately decided to leave, becoming an outcast, and I wasn't the only one. The Queen could be very demanding. And I had other things to fear, too." She changed the subject, gesturing around her. "The rooms are dirty, but there are no more bodies. It's as if they fled suddenly, and were caught outside."

She fell silent again, and Arthur and Finnlugh exchanged a long look full of speculation before Arthur turned and led the way. They were halfway across the next bridge when another volley of arrows and spears rained down from above. The group retreated quickly—all except for Arthur and Tom, who were too far ahead.

An arrow sailed past Tom's ear as they raced to the other side, skidding into the opening unscathed. Tom drew his sword and heard footsteps thundering down the stairs towards them. While Arthur leapt into action, Tom could barely think how to swing his sword and he stabbed wildly, feeling his sword sink into flesh and bone. A sprite swung at his head and, as Tom ducked, the sprite fell dead at his feet. Arthur stood behind him, having barely broken a sweat.

"Are you all right, Tom?"

"I'll let you know later."

Arthur and Tom ran to the top of the stairs and saw several more sprites halfway across the bridge, unaware that they were being watched as they fired on the bridge below. Tom had forgotten how big they were. Their bodies were solid muscle, their flesh a dull greenish-brown, and their faces sharp and angular. Some had horns spiralling out of their skulls, around which their matted hair was wrapped.

Arthur didn't hesitate, and ran silently towards them, his sword held before him. Tom followed hesitantly, his sword also drawn. If he was honest, he didn't feel that he was needed in the battle. Arthur fought with an effortless grace and strength, and his sword looked as if it was an extension of him. He was surefooted and well balanced, and Tom realised clearly, as he hadn't done before, that he was watching Arthur, King of the Britons. He felt a jolt, a sense of unreality that was stronger than anything he'd felt before on this strange journey. The feeling thrust him into the present. He suddenly saw everything with an icy clarity: the vast spanning bridges, the high-walled palace of pitted rock, and the clash of steel.

Tom ran to Arthur's side and helped distract the sprites, attacking one from behind so that he lost his balance and fell from the bridge. Tom's heart was pumping, but he didn't have time to feel afraid. Arthur did all the hard work, and if anything, Tom hoped he wasn't an encumbrance. He jabbed, stabbed, rolled, and ducked repeatedly. When Arthur killed the last sprite, they rolled the bodies off the bridge.

Arthur looked at him, fire in his eyes. "Are you still in one piece?"

Tom was breathless, and adrenalin had him shaking, but he nodded. "I think so. Are you?"

He grinned. "Of course. Never been better." He yelled over the side, "All clear!"

Within seconds the others joined them and they scanned the upper levels again, but the bridges once more appeared empty, the dark entrances in the rock devoid of life, the spindly trees motionless. After hushed reassurances they pressed on, higher and higher.

There were now only eight of them: Arthur, Brenna, Woodsmoke, Finnlugh, Beansprout, and two of the Royal Guard—not many at all, considering what they might encounter at the top, particularly considering Tom and Beansprout had next to no fighting skills. Tom held the sword he had been given, thinking how awkward it felt. He gripped it tighter, wishing his hands didn't feel so sweaty.

When the group reached the final bridge, they stopped to assess their position and share some food to keep them going. Arthur had assumed charge of the small brigade, and no one thought to question his natural command, not even Finnlugh.

They were dizzyingly high. It was freezing, night was falling, and above them was only open sky. The solid walls had gone, and perches lined the latticed walls. The wind moaned, carrying the smell of ice and snow, and patches of drifting mist eddied ceaselessly. Faint stars began to spark and a full moon edged above the forest canopy, lighting the bridge ahead like a ghost road. They could see several armed wood sprites on the other side, their dark silhouettes misshapen and deformed.

"They're guarding the throne room," Brenna informed them.

From the shelter of the doorway, Woodsmoke and the guards exchanged a volley of arrows with the attacking sprites. The sprites aim was good, but they were hampered by both darkness and Woodsmoke's accuracy. If Arthur was master of the sword, Woodsmoke was master of the bow, and eventually the return fire stopped and Arthur led the way across the bridge.

The anteroom was austere and magnificent, its brooding granite walls as smooth as silk, and empty except for the sprites' lifeless bodies.

"Useless brutes," Finnlugh said, kicking one as he strode past.

Arthur paid them greater attention, checking to ensure they were all dead.

Beansprout gingerly stepped over them, grimacing. "It's so eerie here."

Woodsmoke nodded, looking around with interest. "I have heard much about this place, but still, this is not what I was expecting."

"Are they all dead? The court, I mean."

Brenna interrupted, her voice ragged. "I hope not." She laid her hand on the huge double doors of burnished rock and wood that led to the throne room and closed her eyes briefly.

Now that they were finally here, Tom's nerves returned and he asked, "What now?"

Finnlugh's jaw tightened. "We find my brother and claim the Jewel that is rightfully mine."

"Are you prepared for what we'll find in there?" Arthur

asked.

Finnlugh smiled like a shark. "Of course I am. Are you?"

"Always." Arthur turned to Brenna. "Do you think the Queen is in there?"

"No. She would have made her presence felt," she said grimly.

"Well then, Finnlugh, the show is yours. Just ensure you do not put anyone here in danger. Or you'll answer to me."

They stood listening at the door for a few more seconds, but it was deathly quiet, so Arthur turned the handle and pushed open the door.

The throne room was a large square wilderness of cold stone. It was surrounded on three sides by high rocks, and as elsewhere, it was open to the sky. The fourth side, directly opposite the doors, was edged with a low balustrade, beyond which the sky stretched pitilessly. The floor was of smooth stone, and tall, square pillars ran like sentries down either side, creating a ceremonial path to the throne at the far side of the room.

The throne was carved from black granite, and it seemed to suck what little light was left into itself. Crouched in the seat, looking small and insignificant, was the Duke of Craven.

He was focused entirely on a small, glowing object in his hands. It gave off a cold blue light, which flashed occasionally as he turned it. Before the others could even think, Finnlugh swept his hand upwards and pulled the Jewel towards him. It flew from the Duke's grasp, but the Duke responded quickly, throwing his arm to the side. The Jewel, propelled by an unseen force, stopped heading towards Finnlugh and instead clattered against the wall, and then dropped to the floor.

"Tom, get the Jewel!" ordered Finnlugh.

Tom, shocked by the command, stumbled and then ran

to the right to hug the wall, and started edging to the fallen gem. He was vaguely aware of the others fanning out around Finnlugh with their weapons drawn, and he kept an eye on the Duke.

Shocked at their entrance, the Duke jerked upright, fury etched across his face. He glanced at the Jewel and then back at Finnlugh, but before he could react, Finnlugh made a pulling gesture. There was an enormous *crack*, which echoed off the sheer walls, and the throne began to grate across the floor, the grinding of rock against rock sounding like a wounded animal.

In response, the Duke smirked, extending his own hands as he did so. The floor rocked, and Tom crashed to his knees, wincing in pain. Glancing behind him, he saw that only Finnlugh remained standing, and he shouted, "Get back!" to the others, keeping his gaze fixed intently on his brother.

The noise of the grating stone was almost unbearable. Tom pressed his hands to his ears, but unlike the others, who had regained their footing and were edging back to the entrance, Tom ran towards the Jewel, glowing faintly in the distance.

Prince Finnlugh and the Duke were locked together with fierce intensity. Shards of rock began to fly off the throne, shattering against the surrounding walls and cutting Tom's skin like razors. The Duke was closer now, and he leapt from the throne and raced at Finnlugh with shocking speed. He crashed into his brother, and they both rolled across the ground, grappling and punching each other furiously.

Tom tried to protect his head and eyes from the whirling shards of stone and focused only on the Jewel. Just as he was getting close, the ground rocked again and for a moment he thought the floor was dissolving, until he realised that water from an ornamental pool had sloshed across the stone surface. He skidded through it, finally falling in front of the glowing Jewel. He grabbed it quickly before anything else could happen, and looked back towards the Prince.

The far side of the throne room was lost within an ever-expanding, whirling cloud of rocky flints, in the middle of which the fight continued. The moon was now overhead, its light casting monstrous shadows from the pillars, and the floor continued to shudder. Tom had pressed his back against the rock face, seeking shelter, but shale started to slip and slither down the walls, forming rivers of rock, and he realised he couldn't wait any longer. Finnlugh needed the Starlight Jewel before Tom was buried alive.

But before he could move, he heard a screeching laugh overhead, a laugh that grated like fingernails down a blackboard, and he also heard the panic in Brenna's voice as she cried out, "The Queen!"

# Chapter 18: The Old Enemy

A chill entered Tom's heart as he looked up to see a vast, winged figure fly over the hall.

The black shape sped towards them like an arrow, growing in size the closer she came, until the Queen landed with a shake of her immense wings in the centre of the throne room, oblivious to the destruction around her.

Tom froze, wondering what to do. If he ran towards Finnlugh, he risked being seen by the Queen, but without the Jewel, Finnlugh couldn't defeat his brother.

The moonlight cast the Queen's features into sharp lines. Her eyes were black beads set within a long oval face and framed by straight, black hair that swept past her shoulders and down her back. She was semi-human in form, her legs ending in talons that clattered on the floor, and her arms were at her side, a cruel jagged knife in one hand. Wings spread from either shoulder, spanning at least five metres, raising and flexing as she strode past her shattered throne.

"Brenna," she rasped, her voice cruel and hard, "it's been too long. I'm so glad you're back. I've been searching for you, and the others. They think they can hide from me, but they can't hide forever. Come into the light, I want to see you."

Tom watched with horror as Brenna moved forward

from where she had been sheltering at the side of the throne room, as if under a spell. He willed her to run, but although her feet dragged and she clenched her fists, she was drawn irresistibly onwards. Tom looked beyond her, trying to see the others, and hoping that Woodsmoke or Arthur would intervene, but wherever they were, they were hidden in deep shadow, the whirling stones helping to hide them. Tom could only hope that they were waiting for the perfect moment. It was likely Finnlugh hadn't even noticed she'd arrived. He and his brother were still fighting, trading blow for blow.

Brenna stepped out of the shadows of the pillars and into a bright patch of moonlight. She looked up at the Queen, her face etched with fury and fear.

"Did you really think you could come here, and that I would allow you to leave?" The Queen barked out a laugh. "I don't know if you are brave or incredibly foolish."

"Someone reminded me that it was about time that I put a stop to your madness, and he was right. I shouldn't have waited so long."

"But you did, you foolish girl! You're too late now." She looked beyond Brenna to the fighting brothers. "I see the Prince has finally found his brother. Good. I need him to finally control the Starlight Jewel. It will be mine before the night's end, and my power will become absolute." She turned slowly, peering into the shadows, and Tom flattened himself against the ground, hoping she wouldn't see him, but he felt her gaze pierce him like fire, before she turned to Brenna again. "You've brought friends, but they will be of no use. I will kill all of them when I have finished with you. Unless," she smiled, "maybe I should kill one now as a lesson in why you shouldn't betray me! Perhaps the one who currently has the Jewel?"

Tom froze, his heart pounding in his chest, and once again he felt the Queen's gaze settle on him and the Jewel, which pulsed in his hand.

Brenna ignored the threat, drawing the Queen's attention back. "You've done enough killing!" Her voice was steady, despite her fear. "Did you do all this? Did you kill your own people? Your family?"

The Queen stepped closer to Brenna, and with a predatory prowl started to circle around her. "They betrayed me! They refused to do as I asked and then tried to depose me. How could I tolerate that?" Her voice rose higher as her anger increased. "Then they abandoned me and the palace, fleeing to the forest. They left me. Me, their Queen!" She paused and leaned into Brenna's face, her voice now low and dangerous, "And you. You left me years ago, without asking permission."

Brenna lifted her chin, returning the Queen's stare. "You betrayed me, remember? You killed my parents."

The Queen lifted her long, cruel blade and ran it along Brenna's cheek, and a bright line of blood welled up in its wake. "It was a fitting punishment for their crimes. Treason is an ugly thing."

Arthur remained in the shadows, but his voice rang out above the noise that filled the throne room. "And you know all about treason, don't you?"

The Queen turned abruptly, trying to find the source of the voice. "Who is that?"

"You don't recognise me? I'm devastated. I know you. I would recognise that voice anywhere."

She paused, bewildered. "I know who you sound like, but you can't possibly be…"

Arthur had circled behind her, and he called out, "Oh,

but I am."

She whirled around in an effort to see him. "But you are dead. You fell in battle."

"As should you be, Morgan. You've lived well beyond your lifespan."

Tom jolted as he suddenly realised who Queen Gavina really was. *Morgan le Fay, King Arthur's half-sister.*

Morgan didn't seem to care, and she gave a cackling laugh. "Arthur! As if my day couldn't get any better! My half-brother, the apple of my mother's eye, arrives here in my palace!" And then she became deadly serious and her voice thundered across the hall. "How are you here?"

"Merlin's gift, remember? Vivian has brought me back to deal with you."

"That interfering witch! Always messing with things she shouldn't. Just like Merlin!"

"You don't change, do you?" He goaded her, still out of sight. "You're still the selfish, manipulative woman you always were, grubby in your need for power."

"Ha! Says the man who was given power at the moment of his birth!" The Queen had left Brenna's side, and now prowled the hall, looking for Arthur. "For a woman, power does not come so easily. I had to fight for everything! But this world offers many benefits. Others came looking for me after your death, so I made the crossing permanently, to my other home."

"So, while I have been sleeping," he said, as he continued to stalk in the blackest shadows, "you have been meddling and destroying—again."

Her claws clattered on the stone as she stepped towards his voice. "I was going to live quietly here in the forest, but…you know me, Arthur."

Tom glanced between the Queen and the fighting Prince and decided now was his chance to move. He inched down the hall, his heart in his throat, and his hand clasping the Jewel, with half an eye on Morgan and Arthur.

Arthur continued to goad Morgan. "Yes, I do. Unfortunately. You look different. What happened?"

She flexed her wings self-consciously, and for a second Tom sensed regret in her tone. "I had hoped my change in appearance would help me fit in, but things were not as I intended. Magic can be tricky." She tilted her head to one side and looked across to where Prince Finnlugh and the Duke were now fighting with swords, still taunting each other, and then glanced at Brenna, immobile in the centre of the throne room.

"I think you've done enough damage here." Arthur stepped out of the shadows, unexpectedly close to the Queen, and with a flash, plunged Excalibur deep into her side.

She screeched and moved swiftly, hurling Arthur backwards with her wing. "You aren't stronger than me anymore, Arthur," she said, laughing. "Although Vivian obviously thinks so."

With barely a pause, Arthur rolled forward, slashing Excalibur towards her legs. Taking advantage of the distraction, Woodsmoke released a volley of arrows, and the two remaining guards rushed in with their swords raised. Beansprout ran forward to try and pull Brenna back to safety. Most of the arrows bounced off the Queen's wings and onto the floor. One struck deep, but didn't slow her down. As the guards stepped within her reach, she slashed at one with her jagged knife and smashed the other with a powerful sweep of a wing. The first guard collapsed in a pool of blood and the other was swept over the parapet, into the void below. As if to taunt them, she then rose effortlessly out of reach, a biting wind buffeting Tom where he sheltered in the shale. The wound in her side poured with blood, but it didn't seem to be holding her back.

The Queen landed a short distance away, calling out, "Try as hard as you like, you can't save Brenna!" She glared maliciously at Beansprout, and a blast of magic sent her crashing back into the wall, where she collapsed in a heap. Then Brenna screamed and fell to her knees, her shoulders beginning to tear as wings forced their way out.

Tom paused, debating what he could do to distract her. He could make out Morgan's sharp, cruel features and powerful form, and her evil spirit seemed to fill the air. *Should he rush at her? Attack her from behind and try to stab her with his sword?* But if she took the Jewel from him in the struggle, all would be lost.

Arrows flew through the air again, but the Queen used her wings like a shield, and they fell around her, clattering on the floor. Brenna continued her terrifying screams as Arthur ran towards the Queen, his sword raised. But with a wave of her hand, the air around him seemed to solidify, and he stopped as if frozen in place.

The Queen turned back to Brenna. "I shall put you on these walls—a fine decoration for my hall. And then I shall put Arthur next to you."

Tom couldn't let that happen, but the Queen was so powerful… *What could he possibly do?* As water lapped gently in front of him, he remembered the small shell the Emperor had pressed on him before leaving. He pulled it from his pocket and tried to remember what he was supposed do with it. *Something about throwing it in water during times of trouble?* That seemed too easy. But with Brenna now writhing on the floor and the Queen advancing, he needed to act, not doubt himself.

Tom threw the shell into the pool, and it landed with a splash. The ripples spread outwards, gaining in height and intensity until they broke across the floor, and then the water started to froth and boil. The Queen hesitated, looking confused. As she paused, thick grasping tentacles whipped upwards out of the pool, followed by a large, horny head covered in dozens of round, flat eyes. The tentacles grabbed the Queen, enveloping her in their suckered grasp. She screeched and tried to pull free, but the beast had already crushed her wings, and although she tried to stab the creature, she failed, and Tom heard her wings tear from her body as she struggled.

Brenna had now collapsed, seemingly unconscious, and Woodsmoke took advantage of the Queen's immobility and raced to Brenna's side, picked her up, and ran to the door. Arthur was released from the spell, and he ran at the Queen, dexterously avoiding the lashing tentacles, and inflicting as many injuries as he could. But incredibly, the wounded Queen seemed to be freeing herself. Arthur was suddenly caught by a flailing tentacle, and thrown against the wall opposite Tom. They could only watch in horror as the Queen wrestled her captor with increasing strength.

Tom knew he had to get to Prince Finnlugh. He staggered to his feet, wondering how he was going to get the Jewel to him as his attention was so fully focused on the Duke. He shouted, caution suddenly abandoned, "Finnlugh! We need you!"

Finnlugh glanced at Tom, and then behind him, fully focussing on the other fight with the Queen. A new determination crossed his face, and he wrestled the Duke to the ground and extended his right hand. The wind that whirled around them meant that Tom couldn't get any closer, so he threw the Jewel towards Finnlugh's outstretched hand, hoping it would find its way to him through the maelstrom. Finnlugh's break in concentration caused the Duke to push back, and he regained his feet as the Prince staggered.

But as if the Jewel had been summoned to Finnlugh, it snapped into his hand with a sound like a thunderclap.

The Duke howled, "*No!*"

"I told you I would find you and take back my Jewel!" Prince Finnlugh shouted. "Surrender to me while you can."

"Never—you waste your power. It is pointless for you to have it!"

The Duke ran at Finnlugh, but the Jewel pulsed with power, and the Prince blasted a powerful surge of energy at him, sending him crashing into the Queen and the writhing sea creature. A tentacle caught the Duke, wrapping around him and squeezing him tight.

Finnlugh advanced towards them, and Tom recognised the malevolent grin he had seen the night at the Under-Palace. He raised his hand and released the power of the Jewel. Its light grew and expanded, and Prince Finnlugh grew with it until he was as tall as the pillars, blazing with an unearthly brilliance.

"Hold on tight!" Finnlugh shouted as lightning whipped from the Jewel and shot across the hall.

With an immense *crack*, a huge rent opened in the sky above the throne room. Tom felt as if he'd been plunged into the centre of the universe. He could see galaxies and planets swirling in reds, greens, and blues, and could almost taste the cosmic dust that glittered in swathes in the vastness of space.

Then, with a stab of fear, he realised he couldn't breathe. His lungs heaved and he started to rise into the air. He lunged at the closest pillar and gripped tightly, willing himself not to pass out, and he saw Arthur do the same.

The tentacled creature was still wrapped tightly around the Queen and the Duke, and both struggled with increasing terror, but together they rose into the air, and trapped in furious battle, were sucked into the immensity of the universe. Light seemed to be leaking from their every pore, and Tom's last glimpse of the Queen was of one wing breaking free, every tiny feather illuminated by the light beyond it. There was a roar and a shriek, and then utter silence. The night sky returned to normal, and Tom could breathe again.

Tom released the pillar and slumped back to the floor, watching as Finnlugh slowly shrank and collapsed.

It was over; the Queen and the Duke had gone.

*But what about Beansprout, Woodsmoke, and Brenna? How were they?* Tom was about to launch himself to his feet when he saw the doors to the throne room open, Woodsmoke peering through. "All right in there?"

"Just about," Tom said. "Where's Beansprout?"

"She's with us and she's fine, we all are."

Tom slumped back, wondering if any of them would ever be really all right ever again.

# Chapter 19: Legacies and Choices

It was a long night for Tom and the others, perched high above the forest. They crossed to the far side of the bridge and made themselves comfortable in the rooms around the stairway. Arthur gathered wood and made a fire at the start of each bridge, to keep away anything else that might have been lurking in the dark. The flames burned bright and high and took the bitter chill off the air. They gathered blankets and sat around the lower fire, not wanting to look across to the battered throne room.

There were large, bleeding wounds on Brenna's shoulders, caused by the forced expansion of her wings, and an exhausted Finnlugh used the Jewel to heal them. The scars were red and sore, but her pain had eased.

Tom said to Finnlugh, "I'm sorry about your brother."

Finnlugh sighed, his gaze fixed on the flames. "I was furious with him, but I didn't want *that* to happen."

Tom hesitated, wondering what else to say, but Beansprout interrupted. "Well, you shouldn't blame yourself. You did the only thing you could. You saved everyone."

Finnlugh smiled and patted her arm. "Probably the most good I've done in a long time. However, I do seem to have deprived the forest of its Queen." His eyes skimmed over her. "Did she hurt you?"

Beansprout shook her head. "I'm a bit battered, but I'll live. I have the feeling though that the Aerikeen aren't going to miss her much."

Brenna answered, her voice weary. "No, we won't. She was a horrible woman. I should have done something sooner."

"She would have killed you. It was her scheming that killed me," Arthur said.

"Was she really your half-sister?" Finnlugh asked.

"Yes. She was older than me, and shared the same mother. She didn't always resent me," he said sadly. "At one point we actually liked each other, but then … I don't know, she became jealous. She poisoned my nephew against me."

"What a sorry bunch we are," Finnlugh observed. "What with your sister and my brother." He looked at Brenna speculatively. "Who was the Queen to you?"

She didn't say anything for a while, and Tom wasn't sure she was going to answer at all, but then she said softly, "The Queen was my grandmother."

"So, you're the heir?" Finnlugh asked, starting to smile.

"I suppose I am, but it's never been a job I've wanted."

"For the record, I think you'd be excellent at it."

She shook her head. "I think I'd be terrible. I hate affairs of state."

Arthur roused himself, starting to polish his sword. "So did I. I'd have rather been riding into battle than debating policies and politics. What a boring business that was. I delegated as much as I could."

"And how do you feel now that you're here?" Woodsmoke asked him. "Your kingdom has gone."

"And so have my friends," Arthur mused, his face bleak. "But life moves on. I shall find a way forward, I suppose. We all will. For example, what about Tom and Beansprout? What will you do now?"

Beansprout answered straight away. "I'm staying here."

Woodsmoke and Brenna looked startled, and Woodsmoke said, "You are?"

"Yes." She grinned at him, and her whole face lit up. "This is a whole new world to explore. I love it here!"

Tom didn't answer, instead staring into the fire's roaring heart as if the answer to every question could be found there.

"And what will you do, Tom?" Arthur asked, prompting him gently.

"I have no idea. I suppose I should go home, back to the real world."

"This world is real."

"I can vouch for that," Finnlugh said, laughing. "We're not a figment of your imagination."

Tom groaned. "I know, but it's not *my* world."

"But it could be," Arthur pointed out.

Tom glanced resentfully at him. "Now you sound like Beansprout."

"Really? I've always thought she had a lot of sense."

Beansprout preened. "See, Tom!"

Tom ignored her. "So, what are you going to do, Arthur?"

"I have no idea. I might go travelling. I want to see more of this new world I'm living in. I'm excited by its possibilities."

"I forgot that you didn't come from here. You're such a legend, it seems impossible that you ever really existed in our world. In fact, there's nothing to prove you did. It's all just stories."

"*Lots* of stories, though," Beansprout added.

Golden light glinted along Excalibur as Arthur cleaned it. "Well I can assure you it was very real. I lived a whole lifetime. It was only yesterday to me. One day I died, and then you woke me here, albeit a younger version of myself than I appeared on that fateful day."

"Do you actually remember dying?" asked Tom. Then stricken, he added, "Sorry, is that a gruesome question?"

Fortunately, Arthur laughed. "No. I remember being injured and feeling this searing pain, like fire, through my side." He gripped his left side as if to remind himself. "I'd been fighting, and I knew it would probably be my last battle, but even so…" He paused, and his voice dropped. "There was smoke everywhere, thick and choking as if the camp were on fire, and beneath that was the smell of blood. Sweat was stinging my eyes so that I could hardly see, and I was absolutely bone weary and full of sorrow and regret. And there was a lot of shouting, and the horses were screaming. I remember the thudding of their hooves."

For a second, Tom was lost in Arthur's memories, as if he could see it all unfolding around him. "And then?"

"Blackness. Nothingness. Actually—sometimes there were strange dreams, like being at the bottom of a pool looking up through the murky depths. But I think those came later. There was mostly nothing, until you woke me and I rolled out onto the floor of that cave, wondering where I was."

"Did you know about Merlin's deal? That you wouldn't die?"

"Not really. I knew there was something going on, but not what, and to be honest, I didn't care. I had other worries. And I trusted Merlin."

"Do you wish I hadn't woken you?"

"And miss all this? Not many people get two lives, Tom. I shall enjoy it while it lasts. And so should you."

Tom looked up to see all his new friends looking at him, and he fell silent again, having no idea what he would do now.

The next morning, the group walked out of the palace and down the steep cliff path, pausing frequently to rest. The thick, syrupy air of strong magic had gone, but the forest still seemed to bristle around them with a watchful intensity. They were tired after a poor night's sleep, and they mostly walked in silence. When they entered the camp, it was with an air of mourning rather than victory.

Jack welcomed them with relief, and hugged Tom and Beansprout. "Well, thank the Gods, you're all still alive! It's been a horrible night."

"You should thank Prince Finnlugh, he was the one who saved us. It was nothing to do with Gods," Tom said, prying himself out of his granddad's embrace.

Jack carried on, regardless. "That smell caused by the Duchess's spell was so awful, I thought I'd be sick. The wolves came and howled around us for hours, which really upset the horses, and then we saw the lightning shoot from the top of that rock and I nearly had a heart attack."

"I think we all nearly had a heart attack, Granddad," Tom sighed. "At least the smell's gone now," he added reassuringly.

Jack rolled his eyes. "She lifted it at sunrise. She's a funny old bird, Tom!"

"Not half as bad as the funny old bird we met," Tom

grumbled.

Jack burst out laughing. "Good to see you still have your sense of humour after all of this."

It was evening, and they quickly settled themselves around the fire, filling their plates with food as they told the rest of the group about what had happened with Morgan and Duke Craven, when there was a flurry of activity at the edge of the camp. Finnlugh's guards shouted, and they heard muffled responses. Finnlugh and Arthur leapt to their feet, but Brenna was quickest. She ran to the guards, and after a brief explanation they drew back to let a small group of men and women enter the camp. Brenna hugged them all, and after a few brief words, they followed her to the fire.

"These are members of the court," she explained. "Old friends I feared were dead." She turned to them. "Come and join us, have some food."

They were an assortment of the young and old, and all looked weary, although they smiled with relief once they sat and examined everyone—as closely as everyone else looked at them. Tom couldn't help but notice how different they looked from Brenna. Their hair was thick with fine feathers, and markings were clear on their faces, particularly around their eyes, making them look like birds even in their human form.

Brenna sat close to them. "So tell me, are others alive?"

A young man who sat closest to her said, "Yes, we are not the only ones. We've been hiding in remote parts of Aeriken for months, some longer than others. But first, is it true? Is she dead?"

"Yes, Prince Finnlugh came to the rescue," Brenna said, pointing him out. "He blasted her out into the universe."

"Indeed," Finnlugh agreed. "She's somewhere up there,

wrestling with a giant sea creature until the end of time."

"That's quite some trick," one of the younger women said, looking worried.

"Don't worry, *that* trick exhausts me too much to do it often. But it is impressive," he smirked. The Starlight Jewel was now on a long, silver chain around his neck, although buried beneath his clothes, out of sight.

Tom only half-listened as he gazed into the fire, hearing about others who had fled the Queen's wrath, and her increasing insanity. He was thinking of going to bed when a question grabbed his attention. "So, will you stay, Brenna, and help us to bury our dead? And lead us—as Queen?"

Everyone fell quiet, waiting for Brenna's response. She stared into the fire for a long time, and eventually Woodsmoke prompted softly, "Brenna?"

She looked at him and then at the others. "I'll stay to help bury our dead, but then I shall leave. I cannot stay here. It is a place of death. I'll re-join Woodsmoke and live there. That is my home now."

The oldest man in the group spoke next. "But the whole court should move, if you do. We must follow you."

"No! I don't want that." She shook her head. "I'm sorry, but that's the way I feel. And actually, I really don't think you need a King or a Queen. But I will stay for a while."

"I'll stay, too," Woodsmoke offered. "I'll help however I can."

Brenna gave him the ghost of a smile. "No. It's our job, not yours. But thank you."

Finnlugh frowned at her. "You're the heir, they need you."

Her tone was sharp. "I told you, I'm not up to it."

"Wrong," the young woman said. "We don't want

anyone else. But you're grieving, too. So are all of us. Think on it, please."

Brenna nodded, and they fell to talking amongst themselves.

The next day, they all packed up the camp and said goodbye to Brenna and the other Aerikeen.

"Come home when you're ready," Fahey said to her. "I'll miss you."

"You're the sweetest man, and I'll miss you too," she said, tears in her eyes.

Brenna hugged Tom, Beansprout, and Jack, and even Finnlugh. The Duchess merely nodded. "I wish you luck, my dear," was her only comment.

Woodsmoke was less sweet. "You'd better not stay here! This place smells of death. And the wood sprites, they'll be back!"

She shook her head and laughed. "We'll be fine! Now stop moaning and go. I'll see you in a few months." Woodsmoke hesitated, but Brenna persisted. "*Go*! Please Woodsmoke!"

"You're a stubborn woman," he said as he finally relented and got on his horse.

They nudged their mounts and moved off into the forest, and as Tom turned to wave at Brenna, he wondered if he'd ever see her again, and a wave of sadness washed over him.

Days later Tom asked Beansprout, "So, what are we going to do?"

They now rode on their own horses. Finnlugh had spares after the deaths of his men, and he was happy that they should use them. They were huge creatures, but intelligent, and easy to control for inexperienced riders.

Beansprout bristled, preparing herself for another argument. "I've told you, I'm staying."

"To do what?"

"I don't know, Tom! Do I have to have a plan?"

They were now only days away from Woodsmoke's home, and it seemed as if they had been travelling forever. Aeriken was enormous and ancient, and Tom couldn't work out how long it had been since they first arrived.

Jack interrupted. "You should both go. You have your whole lives ahead of you. You belong in your own world."

"You have no right to deliver that speech!" said Tom, rounding on him angrily.

"I have every right—I'm your grandfather!"

"Don't you want us here?"

"I didn't think you wanted to be here. Do you know how contrary you are, Tom?" Jack stared angrily back at him. "And of course I want you to stay. It's nice to have my family here. But I'm not going home," he added, preventing any further questions on that. "I'm an old man there, and here— well, I'm less old."

"Don't you care that Mum and Dad have split up?"

"Of course I care! But my going back wouldn't change anything. They'd still be split up—it's been inevitable for years. And you shouldn't let it affect you. It has nothing to do with you, or what you have or haven't done. It's life, and you should get on with yours. Finish school, travel, enjoy yourself." Jack paused, looking at Tom's mutinous expression. "Just think about the things you've done here. The things you've seen! You're not a child anymore."

Arthur joined in. "If life is unsatisfactory at home, stay here. It sounds like you'd have as much family here as you did there—including me, in case you've forgotten."

Finnlugh interrupted them all. "You speak as if there's only one choice. You could stay for as long as you wanted, and then go when you were ready."

Tom fell silent. *What if he left and then realised he'd made a mistake, and found that he could never come back. What then?*

A peculiar mood had settled over them all. Although they'd known each other for only a short time, they were reluctant to part. Fahey had been badgering them for information, cheerful in the knowledge that he had great tales to craft and share. He and Jack had already arranged to visit Finnlugh's Under-Palace. Arthur had accepted an invitation to stay at Vanishing Hall, but was planning to travel onwards after a short stay. Beansprout and Tom had also been invited, and Beansprout had accepted immediately.

Tom was undecided, and it was tormenting him. He loved his new friends. Woodsmoke was easy going, and a calm, reassuring presence, always willing to teach him how to hunt, track, and use a bow. Fahey was friendly and mischievous, like a teenager in an old fey's body, and Tom now understood why he'd thought that waking King Arthur would be fun. Brenna was cool, and he already missed her. Prince Finnlugh was gracious and entertaining, and ever so slightly reckless, and very grateful for the help in regaining his Starlight Jewel. And of course, there was Arthur.

Tom watched him closely. He'd settled into his new surroundings well, and looked completely at home. He imagined that was because the Otherworld was probably far more like the world he had left than Britain was now. He had an easy grace and humour, and was unfailingly polite and chivalrous to everyone. Beansprout gazed at him, star struck most of the time—as did everyone, actually.

As the days passed, Tom found his original intent to return home waning, and on the night before Finnlugh, the Duchess, and the guards were due to return to the Under-Palace, he had a horribly restless night. They had just passed the huge hawk statues that marked the boundary between Aeriken and Vanishing Wood, and had set up camp together for the final time. Tom had gone to bed late, but couldn't sleep. He tossed and turned and eventually got up and sat by the fire, prodding it back into life, idly watched by one of the guards at the edge of the camp.

Tom sighed as he looked around. What a strange position to be in. He was actually in the Otherworld! A place where fey, dryads, satyrs, and other weird and previously imagined mythical creatures existed. And of course, Arthur and the Lady of the Lake. He couldn't work out why he should stay, but equally, why should he go back? He was still deep in thought when Arthur roused from beneath his blankets, and came and sat next to him.

"Are you all right, Tom?" he asked softly, his voice low so as not to wake the others.

"I have no idea. It's ridiculous, really. I've never been so undecided in my life! I wish I knew how Beansprout can be so sure."

"Because she's following her gut," he explained. "You're overcomplicating things."

"Am I? But there's so much to consider! My whole life is there."

Arthur looked at him, puzzled. "What sort of life? Are you married?"

Tom snorted. "I'm sixteen. Too young to be married!"

"Not in my day," Arthur explained. "We all married young. A woman who wasn't married before she was twenty was thought to be an old maid."

"I can assure you it's very different now!" Tom grimaced, repulsed by the idea of marriage. *What a horrible idea.* "I haven't got a girlfriend either, not really."

Arthur grinned. "Not really?"

Tom shrugged as he thought of Emma at school who he fancied like mad, but only flirted with, badly. "No, definitely not."

"So you'll miss your parents? Of course you will, that's natural."

Tom paused. "Not really. I hardly see my dad, and my mom lives with my sister. I see them every week or so, but I'm probably closest to Granddad, even with him gone for so long. I really missed him when he left."

Arthur persisted. "Do you work?"

"No! I'm at school, final year before college."

"What's college?"

Tom laughed. "Sorry, I forgot you probably had no such thing in your time. It's where teenagers go to school to learn more stuff."

"You like school, then?"

"It's all right," he said, shrugging. "I have no idea what I'm going to do there. I like football, though."

Arthur frowned again. "What's that?"

"The greatest game in the world. I'll show you one day."

"Not if you leave, you won't. Although," Arthur said, scratching his head, "I have to be honest—I'm not sure why you're going back. You don't appear to be going back to anything you'll really miss." Arthur turned away and prodded the fire again, sending a flurry of cinders into the air. "I love fires. They're the best place in the world to think and dream. I'm hoping my life here will be exciting and interesting, but without the responsibilities of leadership and war, and certainly not politics. I hate politics. All that chatter and rhetoric. Don't get me wrong, I loved negotiations, and fighting, and feasting. But sometimes, it was all too much. And having my life threatened all the time was tiring. I'm going to enjoy exploring here, but it would be good to have family to share it with it. Unlike you, I know no one."

"You know us. And I think Granddad and Beansprout are related to you as well, from what Vivian said. And you *do* know her!"

Arthur rolled his eyes in a very un-kingly manner. "Yes I do. She's an annoying woman. I must arrange to meet her at some point, and thank her for my awakening."

As Tom listened to Arthur and his plans, he started to get excited about his own future. *Arthur was absolutely right. What the hell was he rushing to go back for? Absolutely nothing.* He finally had to admit that if he left now, he'd never forgive himself. He smiled, relieved. "Wow. I think you're right."

"Am I? About what?"

"About going back. What a crazy idea! I *should* stay here." He looked at Arthur shyly. "Thank you."

"I have my uses."

"You must have been a good King. No wonder we still talk about you."

Arthur laughed. "You must tell me some of the stories sometime."

"Why don't you tell me one?" Tom prompted. "I've

always been a fan, and have read loads of Arthurian legends. I can tell you if they match up to the real thing!"

Arthur laughed again, looking pleased at being the subject of such speculation. He made himself more comfortable, stretching out his long legs towards the fire. "All right, settle in. What about when my kingship really began, when I pulled the sword from the stone?"

Tom grinned. "Awesome!" He wrapped his cloak around him, and turned to watch Arthur relive his glory days.

As the firelight played across the camp, and the cool night air and sounds from the wood lulled his senses, Tom realised he'd just made the best decision of his life.

Thanks for reading Call of the King. Please make an author happy and leave a review!
Book 2 , The Silver Tower is out now!
Read on for an excerpt!

# THE SILVER TOWER

RISE OF THE KING
BOOK TWO

# TJ GREEN

# Chapter 2: The Hollow Bole

Tom and the others rode into Holloways Meet on a hot, dusty afternoon.

The road broadened and dipped until they reached a large archway formed by thick, interlaced branches. Beyond that, a few small buildings began to appear, built into the high banks of the road. Within a short distance they could hear a steady hum of voices, shouts, laughter, and music, and the banks fell back to form a large, irregular town square dominated by a central group of trees with other Holloways leading into it. It was filled with an assorted collection of beings, young and old, colourful and drab, and the smell of business.

Wooden buildings threaded through the meeting place, some of them perched precariously in branches, others jostling for position on the fields above them, casting deep shadows onto the activities in the centre.

"This place looks busier than ever," Brenna murmured.

"What do people do here?" Tom asked, looking around curiously.

"Many things. I have been told you can buy almost anything here. Consequently, a lot of people pass through, so it's particularly useful for finding out information."

"I love it!" Beansprout declared, her eyes darting

everywhere.

"We'd better find Woodsmoke and Arthur. Woodsmoke said he would try to check into the Quarter Way House," Brenna told them, and pointed to a big building with balconies on the far side of the square, built against the bank and onto the field at the top. "It's more expensive than most inns, but it guarantees a clean bed and good food."

They found Woodsmoke and Arthur sitting in a bar to the side of the main entrance. It was an oasis of calm after the bustle of the square, filled with an assortment of tables and chairs, and screened from the square by thick-limbed climbing plants covered with flowers and a coating of wind-blown dust.

"Well, don't you two look relaxed!" Brenna said, hands on hips.

"The rest of the deserving after a hard day's work!" Woodsmoke smirked as he and Arthur stood to greet them. "Tom—you've grown." He walked around the table and grabbed him in a bear hug, before hugging Beansprout and Brenna. "I've missed you two, too. Look at you, Brenna!" He held her at arm's length, taking in her hair.

"Woodsmoke, it's been only been a few weeks since I last saw you," Brenna said, protesting weakly.

"I don't care. It's good to see you looking like a bird-shifter again!"

Tom had forgotten it had been a while since Woodsmoke had seen Brenna, but he was distracted by Arthur, who crushed him in a hug, too. "You look well, Tom. It's good to have my great-great-great-something relatives join me on Vivian's mad quest." He hugged Beansprout too, lifting her off her feet.

"Are you two drunk?" Beansprout asked, suspicious.

"You're very merry!"

"Can't I just be pleased to see my friends?" Arthur asked, sitting down at the table and picking up his beer again, and gesturing them to sit, too.

Now that he was reunited with all four of his closest friends in the Otherworld—*or anywhere else, really*—Tom felt truly at home. Although Tom had grown in the short time they'd been apart, Woodsmoke and Arthur were both still taller than him—Woodsmoke lean and rangy, his longbow propped next to him at the table, and Arthur muscular, Excalibur in its scabbard at his side.

"Let's get more drinks to celebrate," Arthur suggested, and called to the barman. "Five pints of Red Earth Thunder Ale, please!"

As they sat, Beansprout asked, "So, how long have you been here?"

"It took us longer to get here than we thought," Woodsmoke answered. "We wanted to make sure none of the other villages had seen Nimue, so we only arrived here this morning, and decided we needed to recover after our long days on the road." He paused as their ale arrived, and took a long drink as if to emphasise his need to recuperate.

Arthur nodded. "Yes, I wasn't entirely sure Vivian had given us accurate information, but it seems for once, she has. And she's suggested that Nimue stayed at The Hollow Bole—apparently, it's where she's stayed before. That's where I'll be going soon, to ask a few questions." He looked at Tom. "Do you want to come?"

"Yes," Tom said, spluttering his drink in an effort to answer. "But first, tell me what happened with Vivian."

"Ah!" Arthur said, gazing into his pint, "Vivian. It was very strange to meet her again, after so many years. I felt quite sick seeing that big, bronze, dragon-headed prow gliding out of the mist." He sighed, trying to organise his story. "I met her by the lake, at her request. I'd wanted to contact her, but didn't know how. I thought that standing at the lakeside, yelling into the mist probably wouldn't work. But then I had these images enter my dreams, about the standing stones and the lakeside."

"Oh, yes," Tom interrupted. "I've experienced those!"

"So I headed to the lake, and within an hour the boat was there, and then almost instantly she was at my side. She looked so old, and yet so young." He looked up at the others, as if trying to make them see what he had. "I couldn't believe her hair was white! It used to be a rich dark brown that glinted with red when it caught the sunlight. She had freckles then, all over her nose and cheeks." He shook himself out of his reverie as his friends watched him, fascinated by what he must be remembering. "She asked me if I remembered her sisters, the other priestesses, particularly Nimue, which I did. Nimue helped me rule when Merlin disappeared. Vivian explained that she had vanished on her way to Dragon's Hollow to see Raghnall, the dragon enchanter—whoever he is. She was taking her time, visiting various people along the way. The last time Vivian heard from her was when she was here. It's another week's travel to Dragon's Hollow, but she never arrived there."

"And how does Vivian know she hasn't arrived?" Beansprout asked.

"Because Raghnall contacted Vivian, by scrying, to find out where Nimue was. Apparently, Vivian has been trying to contact her ever since, also by scrying, which is apparently how they communicate long distance. Now, Vivian thinks she's being blocked, either by Nimue or someone else."

"What's Nimue like?" Tom asked.

"Oh, she's very different to Vivian. She's small and dark-haired, like a pixie, very pretty. Merlin was infatuated with her," Arthur said thoughtfully. "Vivian is worried that something is wrong, so we've spent the last few days trying to track her route, but we've found nothing of interest. It all seems a wild goose chase," he said, finishing his pint. "So, Tom, shall we go? Woodsmoke looks too comfortable to move." He frowned at Woodsmoke, who had his feet up on a chair looking very relaxed.

"It's been a busy few weeks," Woodsmoke said, indignant. "And I'm much older than you are, so I deserve to relax. Besides, I also have news to catch up on," he added, gesturing to Brenna and Beansprout. He waved them off. "Enjoy your afternoon."

Tom and Arthur set off on a slow, circuitous route.

"I know I've been here a few months now, Tom, but I still can't get used to the place."

Tom nodded. "I know what you mean. Everything is so odd!"

Strange creatures bustled across the square, some tall, others small, male and female, some part human, part animal. They passed a group of satyrs and felt small by comparison. The satyrs were over seven feet tall, with muscular bodies, their upper half bare-chested, the lower half with the hairy legs of goats. Their hair was thick and coarse, large curling rams' horns protruded from their heads, and their eyes were a disconcerting yellow that made them look belligerent. Tom and Arthur skirted past them, making their way to a row of buildings at the side of the square. These were a mixture of shops, semi-permanent markets, eating places, and inns, ranging from the small and shabby to the large and less shabby. Smoke from braziers drifted through the still air. They looked at the wooden signs that hung from the entrances, trying to find The Hollow Bole.

The pair had been looking for nearly an hour, taking their time drifting through the warren of buildings, before they had any joy. Walking down the start of one of the Holloways, they saw a vast tree to their left, pressing against the bank at its back. There was a narrow cleft in its trunk, above which a small sign announced *The Hollow Bole*. Peering upwards through the leaves, they saw small windows scattered along thick and misshapen branches. Ducking to avoid hitting their head on the low entrance, they stepped into a small hall hollowed out of the trunk and followed the narrow, spiralling stairs upwards into the gloom. They emerged into a larger hall built into a broad branch overlooking the Holloway and the edge of the square. There were no straight lines anywhere. Instead, the chairs, tables, and balcony were an organic swirl of living wood.

A dryad, green-skinned and willowy, stepped out of the shadows and asked, "Can I help you?"

Thinking they were alone, Tom jumped. Arthur remained a little more composed and said, "I'm looking for an old friend who passed through here, probably a few weeks ago now. Can you confirm if she stayed here?"

"And what do you want with this friend?" the dryad snapped.

"She hasn't arrived where she should have, and I want to find out if anything has happened to her," Arthur replied, trying to keep the impatience out of his voice.

The dryad went silent for a moment. "It depends who it is. Her name?"

"Nimue. Our mutual friend, Vivian, asked me to find

her. She's worried."

The dryad was startled. "Nimue? The witch?" She spat out *witch* viciously.

Now Arthur was startled. "Yes, Nimue, one of the priestesses of Avalon. Or *witch*, as you choose to call her."

"They are all witches on Avalon," the dryad replied disdainfully. "Yes, she stayed here for a few days. And then she left. I don't know where she went," she added, to avoid further questions.

Arthur groaned. "She gave no indication at all of where she might be going?"

"She stays here because we are discreet. We ask no questions of our clients."

"But you know her well? She stays here often, I believe."

"Not often. She travels less frequently now. But yes, I think she usually stays here. However, I do not know her well. I do not ask questions."

Tom was curious about the word *now*, and clearly Arthur was, too.

"But she used to travel here more frequently? In the past?" Arthur persisted.

The dryad was visibly annoyed at the constant questions. "Yes, many years ago. But, I do not see what that has to do with now—and I was not here then."

"So if you weren't here then, how do know she came here?" Arthur asked.

"Her name appears in our past registers. We are an old establishment. And her reputation precedes her."

Now Arthur was clearly very curious, and he leaned in. "What reputation?"

"As a witch from another world. A meddler in the affairs of others."

"What affairs?"

"Witches meddle with the natural order of nature!" the dryad snapped, now furious. "As a dryad, I am a natural being, born of the earth and all her darkest mysteries. Witches plunder that knowledge! They have no respect for natural laws. How do *you* know her?"

Arthur looked uncomfortable, and decided not to answer that. "I am just an old friend who cares for her safety. I am sorry to have taken so much of your time. Are you sure you don't remember anything else?"

"Nothing."

"Just one more question. Did she ever stay here with anyone else?"

"Yes. The greatest meddler of them all—Merlin." With that, she stepped back into the shadows and melted into the tree trunk, becoming invisible and unreachable.

"With Merlin?" Arthur turned to Tom dumbfounded, his face pale at this unexpected news.

Tom felt a thrill run through him at the mention of Merlin, but why was Arthur so upset? Before he could ask, Arthur turned and raced down the stairs. Tom raced after him. *Maybe it was because Merlin had travelled here, to the Meet,* Tom reflected. *It was probably quite unexpected.*

Arthur was halfway back to the Quarter Way House before Tom caught up with him. "Arthur, what's the matter?"

"Everything!"

"What do you mean, *everything?*" Tom asked, even more confused.

Arthur didn't answer, and instead headed to their inn, ran up the stairs, and banged on what Tom presumed was their shared room door.

"Yes? I'm here and I'm not deaf! Come in, the door's

open."

But Arthur was already in, throwing the door wide open and striding across the room.

"What's the matter with you?" Woodsmoke asked, alarmed. He was sitting on a chair on the small balcony overlooking the square.

Tom followed Arthur, closing the door behind him, while Arthur sat agitatedly beside Woodsmoke. "Nimue used to come here with Merlin."

Looking confused, Woodsmoke asked, "Is that good or bad?"

"I don't know," Arthur said, confused. "Both? Neither? It's just odd. It's a shock, that's all."

"But this was a long time ago? She wasn't here with him recently?" Woodsmoke asked.

"No, no, of course not. He disappeared years ago. Well, not so long ago for me, merely a few years. But even so, it's a surprise."

"Why? You said they knew each other."

"Yes, but to know that they were *here*! *Together*! I didn't think she liked him. She actively avoided him at first, I think." Arthur looked troubled as he tried to recall the nature of their relationship.

"So, you're shocked because you didn't think they knew each other well?" Woodsmoke asked, trying to get to the root of Arthur's problem, and looking further confused in the process.

"Yes," Arthur said. "And now it seems they knew each other better than I realised. Merlin had a sort of obsession with Nimue, but she used to keep him at a distance. Of course, he was much older than her at the time, an old man. A very grumpy, unkempt old man. Still powerful, of course.

And she was young and very beautiful. I saw her more often than Vivian—she represented Vivian and Avalon at Camelot. It was there that Merlin first met her." Arthur gazed into the middle distance as he tried to remember the details. "But he could be charming. And he never stopped trying to impress her."

"So, maybe he finally managed to charm her into friendship."

"Maybe. I think she was impressed with his powers, if nothing else. Perhaps that's what swayed her? Maybe they *did* become good friends?" he mused.

"What powers did Merlin have?" Tom asked. He sat on the floor of the balcony, leaning back against the railing, watching the exchange.

"He was a shape-shifter. He favoured fish and stags, but he could turn into anything he chose. And he had the power of prophecy. But he could perform other magic and spells. I gather he learnt much from travelling here. Obviously, the dryad at The Hollow Bole did not approve of either Merlin or Nimue."

Woodsmoke looked puzzled. "Why not?"

"She said they meddled in the natural order. She seemed to prize her own natural magical abilities far more highly."

"Maybe because their magic is acquired. And of course, they are human."

"Perhaps. Although, I believe Merlin was born with his powers of prophecy and shape-shifting. The rumours were that nobody knew who his father was." Arthur shrugged. "I don't know. Merlin always guarded his secrets closely. He didn't like to share where he was going or what he was doing."

"Perhaps he bewitched Nimue?" Woodsmoke asked.

Arthur looked up sharply. "No, I find that hard to believe. Although," he said thoughtfully, "he was not averse to doing things that would benefit him." He shot off his chair and paced up and down. "You cannot understand how odd this is for me! I have been dead—or asleep, whatever you choose to call it—for hundreds and hundreds of years, but for me that time was only months ago. And yet all of my friends are dead and buried, my kingdom has disappeared, my home is gone, and I am a myth! It's as if I never existed, as Beansprout and Tom told me." He gestured vaguely in Tom's direction. "No evidence that I ever existed at all! As if I am a mere shadow. But then I find that Vivian is still alive, that Morgan was alive, albeit in some other form, and now Nimue! Such unnatural lifespans! And Merlin disappeared hundreds of years ago, but the dryad spoke as if he had just left the room." Deflated, he sat down again. "I don't think I will ever get used to this."

Woodsmoke seemed to take this outburst in his stride, as if he expected it. "I'm sorry, Arthur. I can only imagine how confusing this must be for you. But I thought you liked your chance at another life?"

"I did, and I suppose I still do, most of the time. But today has made me reconsider. However, there isn't much I can do about it. This is my fate, and I must live with it."

End of Excerpt

# Author's Note

*The Call of the King* is a rewrite of *Tom's Inheritance*, which was my very first book! I'm very fond of the Tom series, and I've rewritten it because I decided that it could be better. I've learned a lot since publishing it, and realised it needed smoothing out, and needed a different ending.

The rest of the story hasn't changed dramatically, but I'm pleased with all the changes I've made, and now feel that I've done Tom justice.

I decided to rebrand the entire series, so all of the books have new titles, a new series title, and new covers!

As I've changed the ending to *Call of the King*, there are small changes to the beginning of book two. It was called *Twice Born*, but is now called *The Silver Tower*. Book three, previously called *Galatine's Curse*, is now *The Cursed Sword*, and the story is completely unchanged.

This book initially took me five years to write, in between working full-time and studying for my English degree. I'm pleased to say that I write much quicker now!

I love the King Arthur tales, and this is my own retelling. It seems natural to have King Arthur awake in the Otherworld, because his stories have always crossed over with fey and dragons, magic and mystery. I hope you've enjoyed my spin on them.

Thanks to my fabulous cover designer, Fiona Jayde Media, my first editor, Sue Copsey, who was fantastic in whipping the original into shape, and thanks to Missed Period Editing, who have tidied up this second version.

I owe a big thanks to Jason, my partner, who has been incredibly supportive throughout my career, and was a beta reader. Thanks also to Terri and my mother, my other two beta readers. You're all awesome.

Finally, thank you to my launch team, who give valuable feedback on typos and are happy to review on release. It's lovely to hear from them—you know who you are! You're amazing! I also love hearing from all my readers, so I welcome you to get in touch.

If you'd like to read a bit more background to the stories, please head to my website, where I blog about the books I've read and the research I've done. I have another series set in Cornwall about witches, called White Haven Witches, so if you love myths and magic, you'll love that, too. It's an adult series, not YA.

If you'd like to read more of my writing, please join my mailing list. You can get a free short story called *Jack's Encounter*, describing how Jack met Fahey—a longer version of the prologue in *The Call of the King*—by subscribing to my newsletter. You'll also get a FREE copy of *Excalibur Rises*, a short story prequel.

You will also receive free character sheets on all of my main characters in White Haven Witches—exclusive to my email list!

By staying on my mailing list, you'll receive free excerpts of my new books, as well as short stories and news of giveaways. I'll also be sharing information about other books in this genre you might enjoy. I also welcome you to join my readers' group for even more great content, called TJ's Inner Circle on Facebook. Please answer the questions to join! https://business.facebook.com/groups/696140834516292/

Give me my FREE short stories by subscribing here: https://tjgreen.nz/landing/

# About the Author

I write books about magic, mystery, myths, and legends, and they're action packed!

My new series is adult urban fantasy, called White Haven Witches. There's lots of magic, action, and a little bit of romance.

My YA series, Rise of the King, is about a teen named Tom and his discovery that he is a descendant of King Arthur. It's a fun-filled, clean read with a new twist on the Arthurian tales.

I've got loads of ideas for future books in both series, including spin-offs, novellas, and short stories, so if you'd like to be kept up to date, subscribe to my newsletter. You'll get free short stories, character sheets, and other fun stuff. Interested? Subscribe here.

I was born in England, in the Black Country, but moved to New Zealand 14 years ago. England is great, but I'm over the traffic! I now live near Wellington with my partner, Jase, and my cats, Sacha and Leia. When I'm not busy writing I read lots, indulge in gardening and shopping, and I love yoga.

Confession time! I'm a Star Trek geek—old and new—and love urban fantasy and detective shows. My secret passion is Columbo! My favourite Star Trek film is The Wrath of Khan, the original! Other top films for me are

Predator, the original, and Aliens.

In a previous life, I was a singer in a band, and used to do some acting with a theatre company. On occasions, a few friends and I like to make short films, which begs the question, Where are the book trailers? I'm thinking on it…

For more on me, check out a couple of my blog posts. I'm an old grunge queen, so you can read about my love of that here. For more random news, read this.

Why magic and mystery?

I've always loved the weird, the wonderful, and the inexplicable. My favourite stories are those of magic and mystery, set on the edges of the known, particularly tales of folklore, faerie, and legend—all the narratives that try to explain our reality.

The King Arthur stories are fascinating because they sit between reality and myth. They encompass real life concerns, but also cross boundaries with the world of faerie—or the Otherworld, as I call it. There are green knights, witches, wizards, and dragons, and that's what I find particularly fascinating. They're stories that have intrigued people for generations, and like many others, I'm adding my own interpretation.

I also love witches and magic, hence my second series set in beautiful Cornwall. There are witches, missing grimoires, supernatural threats, and ghosts, and as the series progresses, even weirder stuff happens.

Have a poke around in my blog posts and you'll find all sorts of posts about my series and my characters, and quite a few book reviews. If you'd like to follow me on social media, you'll find me here: Facebook, Twitter, Pinterest, Instagram.

Printed in Great Britain
by Amazon